How God Used A

SNOWDRIFT

How God Used A
SNOWDRIFT
And Other Devotional Stories

Joel R. Beeke & Diana Kleyn
Illustrated by Jeff Anderson

CHRISTIAN FOCUS PUBLICATIONS

© copyright 2003 Reformation Heritage Books
Published by Christian Focus Publications
and Reformation Heritage Books
ISBN: 1-85792-817-2
Christian Focus Publications Ltd,
Geanies House, Fearn, Tain,
Ross-shire, IV20 1TW.
Scotland, Great Britain
www.christianfocus.com
email: info@christianfocus.com
Reformation Heritage Books
2919 Leonard St, NE, Grand Rapids, MI, 49525
Phone: 616-977-0599
Fax: 616-285-3246
email: RHBookstore@aol.com
Website: www.heritagebooks.org
Illustrations and Cover illustration by Jeff Anderson
Cover design by Alister Macinnes
Printed and bound in Great Britain by
Cox & Wyman

Building on the Rock · Book titles and Themes
Book 1: How God used a Thunderstorm
Living for God and The Value of Scripture
Book 2: How God stopped the Pirates
Missionary Tales and Remarkable Conversions
Book 3: How God used a Snowdrift
Honoring God and Dramatic Deliverances
Book 4: How God used a Drought and an Umbrella
Faithful Witnesses and Childhood Faith
Book 5: How God Sent a Dog to save a Family
God's Care and Childhood Faith

Acknowledgements

All of the Christian stories contained in these books are based on true happenings, most of which occurred in the nineteenth century. We have gleaned them from a variety of sources, including several books by Richard Newton, then rewrote them in contemporary language. Many of them are printed here for the first time; others were previously printed, without the accompanying devotional material, in a series titled *Building on the Rock* by the Netherlands Reformed Book and Publishing and by Reformation Heritage Books in the 1980s and 1990s.

Thanksgiving is rendered to God first of all for His help in preparing this series of books. Without Him we can do nothing. We would also like to thank James W. Beeke for supplying some helpful material; Jenny Luteyn, for contributing several of the stories; Jeff Anderson for his illustrations; and Catherine MacKenzie, for her able and invaluable editing. Finally, we would like to thank our loyal spouses, Mary Beeke and Chris Kleyn, for their love, support, and encouragement as we worked on these books over several years. We pray earnestly that the Lord will bless these stories to many hearts.

Joel R. Beeke and Diana Kleyn
Grand Rapids, Michigan

Contents

How to use this book

The stories within this book and the other titles in the *Building on the Rock* series are all stories with a strong gospel and biblical message. They are ideal for more than one purpose.

1.   Devotional Stories: These can be used as a child's own personal devotional time or as part of family worship.

Please note that each story has at least one scripture reference. Every story has a scripture reading referred to at the end which can be used as part of the individual's or the family's Bible reading program. Many of the stories have other references to scripture and some have several extra verses which can also be looked up.

Each story has two prayer points at the end of the book. These are written as helps to prayer and are not to be used as prayers themselves. Reading these pointers should help the child or the family to think about issues connected with the story that need prayer in their own life, the life of their church or the world. Out of the two prayer points written for each story, one prayer point is written specifically for those who have saving faith while the other point is written in such a way that both Christians and nonbelievers will be brought to pray about their sinful nature and perhaps ask God for his salvation or thank him for his gift of it.

Each story has also a question and discussion section at the end where the message of the story can either be applied to the reader's life or where a direct question is asked regarding the story itself or a related passage of scripture. The answers to the direct questions are given at the end of the book. Scripture references are indexed at the back of the book. Beside each chapter number you will read the scripture references referred to. These include references within the story, question or scripture reading sections.

2.   *Children's Talks:* As well as all the features mentioned above, the following feature has a particular use for all those involved in giving children's talks at Church, Sunday School, Bible Class, etc. At the end of the series in Book 5, you will find a series index of scripture in biblical order where you will be able to research what books in the series have reference to particular scriptures. The page number where the scripture appears is also inserted. Again, all scriptures from stories, question sections, and scripture readings are referred to in this section

It is also useful to note that each book will have a section where the reader can determine the length of specific stories beforehand. This will sometimes be useful for devotional times but more often will be a useful feature for those developing a children's talk where you are very dependent on the time available.

Shorter Length Stories
The following stories are shorter in length than the average length of story included in this book. They therefore may be used for family devotions, children's talks, etc. where not so much time is available:

Longer Length Stories

The following stories are longer in length than the average length of story included in this book. They therefore may be used for family devotions, children's talks, etc. where more time is available:

1. A Barber Receives His Reward

Many years ago there lived a barber in the city of Bath, England. For a long time he had been in the habit of keeping his shop open on Sunday. But after he became a Christian, he believed that he was breaking the Sabbath and that he must close his barber shop on Sundays. Yet, he was afraid to do so. He thought if he did so, he would offend his customers and lose all his business.

The barber went to ask the minister about his problem. The minister advised him to close his shop on the Sabbath and trust God to take care of him.

He did so. He hung out a sign that said "Closed Sundays," and tried to trust God to take care of him. But it turned out as the barber feared. His customers were offended. Because he would not shave them and cut their hair on Sunday, they refused to come to him during the week. He was forced to give up his fashionable shop and open up a shop in a dingy basement where he had hardly enough business to get himself bread to eat.

Well, what then? Did God's promise fail in the case of this poor barber? Did he suffer loss by closing his shop on the Sabbath for the sake of Jesus? Wait a little, and see!

One Saturday evening, just as it was getting dark, a strange gentleman, who had just arrived by coach, asked for a barber. One of the drivers pointed to the cellar across the street. He came in hastily, and asked for a quick shave and a haircut while they were changing horses, as it would be too late at night when he reached the end of his journey, and he did not like to break the Sabbath. This touched the barber's feelings, so that he could not help weeping. He asked the stranger to lend him a penny to buy a candle, as it was not light enough to work. The gentleman gave it, pitying the great poverty of the poor barber.

When the barber was finished, the stranger said, "It seems to me, my friend, that there is something unusual in your past, and I'd like to hear about it, but I really must go now. Here is some money for your services. When I come back this way I would like to visit you again. What is your name?"

"William Reed."

The gentleman looked startled, and exclaimed, "William Reed? Are you from the west of England?"

"Yes, sir; from Kingston, near Taunton."

"What was your father's name?"

"Thomas."

"Did he have a brother?"

"Yes, sir; one, after whom I was named.

But he went to the East Indies, and as we never heard from him, we suppose him to be dead."

"You must come with me," exclaimed the gentleman. "I am going to see a person who claims to be William Reed, of Kingston, near Taunton. If you can prove that he is an imposter, and you are the person I am seeking, I have some amazing news for you. Your uncle died recently, and has left an immense fortune, which I will hand over to you, as soon as I am sure that you are the William Reed I am seeking."

The barber went with the gentleman. He had no difficulty proving that he was the real William Reed, and his uncle's large fortune was soon put into his possession.

How amazing this was! God brought it about in such a way as to reward him for his faithfulness. When he decided to close his shop on Sunday, he was doing it for the Lord. It seemed, at first, as if he was going to suffer a great loss for what he had done. But, in the end, he was rewarded more than a hundredfold. For, if he had not closed his shop on Sundays, he would not have lost his customers. And if he had not lost his customers, he would not have been in that cellar, so poor as to have to beg a penny for a candle. And if it had not been for this, the gentleman who was in charge of his uncle's fortune would not have discovered who he was.

Children, this is a very remarkable story.

I do not want you to think that God rewards all of His children with great amounts of money; God's children must serve and obey Him out of love for God. They must be willing, as this barber was before he became rich, to obey God no matter what the cost. You must remember that God's children can also be truly happy and content even if they are very poor, or in great pain, or in great trouble. The lesson in this story is that we must obey God, even when things do not seem to go right. God wants our whole heart, and He is worthy of it!

Question: Can you remember which of the Ten Commandments the barber was keeping when he refused to work on the Lord's day?
Scripture reading: Luke 18:28-30.

2. A Captain's Regret

Captain Pierson commanded a large merchant ship which carried goods from one country to another. On one voyage, he saw a distress signal. Looking through the "spy-glass," he could make out some people on the deck of a sinking ship.

"Shall we change course, sir, and help them?" asked the first mate.

"No! We shall not change our course," replied Captain Pierson.

The crew was shocked. When they came closer to the ship, they could hear the cries for help. They begged their captain to help the poor people. But he refused. He would not stop and help the drowning people.

Why did he not want to help them? Usually, captains and sailors hurry to help those in need. Let me tell you why. It was his love of money. His ship was loaded with good cargo. He knew he could make a lot of money with the goods on his ship. The problem was, that another ship had left England the same day he had, carrying the same cargo. It was headed to New York, just as he was. If he got there first, he would sell his goods first, and make more money.

So, the captain did not change his

course. He left the crew and passengers of the sinking ship to drown in the ocean. Before the end of the voyage, he made each crew member promise never to tell about the sinking ship they had neglected.

Captain Pierson became very rich from the sale of his cargo, but he lived and died a miserable man. He could never forget that sinking ship and the poor people who went down with it. The thought of it tortured him by day and filled his dreams at night. He had a splendid house by the seashore, but when storms swept by, he would be reminded of the shrieks of the drowning crew and passengers of that ship.

You must ask the Lord to give you a new heart. Then you will not be slaves to the things of this world. Ask the Lord if you may belong to Him, and to make you useful in His service. Serving sin and the world brings no joy or satisfaction, but serving the Lord out of love to Him, gives you peace. "Good understanding giveth favor: but the way of transgressors is hard" (Proverbs 13:15).

Question: The Captain was determined to make money but can you think of one woman in the Bible who gave all the money that she had to God? (Mark12:42)
Scripture reading: 1 Timothy 6:3-16.

3. A Child's Answer

A man walking in a park noticed a boy reading a book. "What are you reading?" asked the gentleman.

"A New Testament, sir," answered the boy with a smile. "I got it for my birthday."

"Do you believe that there is a God?"

"Yes," replied the boy with surprise. "I know there is a God."

The man wanted to make fun of the boy and asked, "Is your God little or great?"

After thinking for a moment, the boy said, "He is both."

"And how can that be?" laughed the man.

"Well," explained the boy, "God is so little that He can come and live in my wicked heart, yet He is so great that the whole world cannot hold Him."

What a wise answer for a mocking man! The boy was not ashamed to say that he believed in God. If you believe in God, then you will obey His commands and repent from your sins. Do not delay. Go immediately to the Lord Jesus Christ for salvation.

Question: What would you answer if someone asked you if you believe in God? How could you prove your answer?
Scripture reading: 1 Kings 8:22-30

4. A Child's Gift

A little girl named Katy was the daughter of a poor widow. At Sunday School she heard a missionary tell about heathen children living in sin and misery, never having heard the gospel. When he talked about the importance of sending Bibles to them, Katy said to herself, "I want to help."

When she came home, she told her mother what she had heard. That night she lay in bed thinking about the children who had never heard about the Lord Jesus. So the next morning, she went to her mother and asked, "Is Pet mine to keep?"

"Yes, dear," answered her mother. "it is."

Pet was a little motherless chicken, about a month old, which a neighbor had given Katy. Katy loved it very much. Pet knew Katy's voice and followed her everywhere. It was the little girl's treasure.

"Mommy," began Katy, "I am going to give Pet to the missionary. I have nothing else to give, and I am going to carry it to the minister's this morning."

Katy's mother smiled. "What a good idea, Katy. I am glad you care so much about what the missionary told you."

Katy went out to give Pet its last breakfast, and as the crumbs fell from her hand, her eyes filled with tears. But she got a basket, lined it with a soft cloth, and put Pet in it. When she told the minister her story, tears filled the man's eyes, too. He could not help thinking that if his whole congregation had Katy's giving spirit, they would be able to raise a good sum of money for the mission. He gave Katy some money for the chicken which she then solemnly dropped in the missionary box on the minister's table. Sadly, she turned to leave.

"Katy," said the minister.

"Yes, sir," answered Katy with a quiver in her voice.

"I have no one to take care of this little chick. Would you like to take it home and take care of it for me?"

Katy's face broke into a happy smile. "Really? Oh, I would love to!"

Gently she placed Pet back in the basket and thanked the minister. Home she went, her heart overflowing with double gladness.

Question: What can you give to help God's work? Most importantly, have you surrendered your life to Jesus? What does 1 Chronicles 29:14 teach us about the money and other things that we give to help God's cause and people?
Scripture readings: Luke 21:1-4; Romans 12:1-21.

5. A Sunday Boat Trip

David lived in England. His parents taught him always to be in church on Sunday. One day his friends invited him to go boating on the next Sunday afternoon. David's conscience warned him, but he wanted to please his friends so David decided to go.

That Sunday, the weather was beautiful. David and his friends planned to sail down the Thames River. Suddenly, David's conscience spoke, "Remember the Sabbath Day to keep it holy!" (Exodus 20:8) He hesitated and then told his friends he would not go. They laughed at him and left him standing on the dock. David felt terrible. How could he answer them if they would tease him the next day about not going along? However, the boys in the boat became careless. Before the afternoon had ended, they ran into a barge full of coal. Their boat sank and six of David's friends drowned in the river. What thoughts and feelings do you think filled the heart of David?

Question: What does 2 John 9 tell us about those who transgress.
Scripture reading: Daniel 6.

6. Beth's Obedience

Beth Schultz lived in a small town in Germany. Her father and mother were very well-known and had many friends. But they never attended church; they lived very worldly lives. For this reason, Beth's life was very difficult.

When Beth was a little girl, she went to church with some friends. The Lord blessed the service to her heart, and she learned about the way of salvation. From then on, Beth went to church whenever she could. This made her parents very angry. One day Mr. Schultz said, "Beth, you are wasting your time with this foolishness. Promise me that you will never go to church again!"

Beth loved her parents very much but she loved the Lord even more. "I'm sorry to disobey you, Father," she answered, "but God's command is that I must obey Him." This made her father angry, but Beth continued to attend church, trusting that the Lord would care for her.

One evening Beth returned home from church to find the house full of noisy, laughing people. Her parents were holding a dance at their home. As she entered by a back door, her father spotted her. "Ah, Beth, you are finally here! You are just in time to join the next dance."

Beth could tell that her father was determined, yet she tried to be excused. "Please excuse me, Father. I have just attended a church service. It would be very wrong for me to go from church to a dance!"

"I don't care if you were in church again! I insist that you go in and dance. If you do not, I will punish you severely!"

"Please, Father," she begged, "don't make me go in. I will do anything you wish that is right."

Hearing this, her father became very angry. "I won't listen to any more excuses!" As he spoke, he took her by the arm and forced her into the room where the dance was being held. When Beth saw the dancers whirling around the room, she turned pale. Everyone saw her enter, and she wondered how she could make her escape. Dan, one of the wildest boys in town, was also there. Before she knew what happened, he came to her and politely asked, "May I please have the next dance with you?"

Now Beth faced a most difficult decision. Everyone curiously watched to see what she would do. The room grew very quiet. Would she deny her confession? Would she choose to serve Christ or the world?

Beth hesitated for only a moment. Then she fell down on her knees and cried out,

"Lord, help me! Lord, deliver me! Thou knowest that I may not dance! Thou knowest that I desire to serve Thee! Save me, oh, save me, for Christ's sake!"

Beth's prayer was heard. Everyone was stunned and it remained deathly quiet for a moment. But Harry, one of the musicians, was deeply touched by this scene. Overpowered by what he saw, he smashed his violin to the floor. "I have served Satan for many years," he cried, "but I will serve him no more!" From that time on, Harry's life was changed. Beth's prayer proved to be the means of his conversion, and Harry learned to serve the Lord. Beth's prayer was also the end of the dance. The trap her father had set for her had failed. She had bravely taken a stand for Jesus and had won the victory. The Lord had made it true for her that "They that honor me, I will honor." (1 Samuel 2:30)

But Beth's father was displeased. His anger turned to hatred for his faithful daughter. Each time she went to church his hatred burned deeper. One night he formed a hateful plan. Rex, his German shepherd, was a large, vicious dog who faithfully obeyed his master. Mr. Schultz now called his dog and they went off into the darkness to wait for Beth to return from church. Finally he saw her coming and waiting until she was nearly in front of him, he gave the command, "Go get her, Rex!"

Rex immediately sprang upon his victim, obeying the command of his master. Beth could not recognize the dog, for it was dark. But throwing her arms up to protect her face, she cried out, "Help! Help me! Down, boy! Help!" Rex recognized her voice at once, and his growls changed to a happy bark. He licked his mistress and ran in circles around her, barking happily. Now Mr. Schultz's anger knew no limits. Seeing that his plan had failed again, he sprang up from beside the road. Looking wildly around, he grabbed a heavy stick and began to beat poor Beth. At last he threw his stick away and left her.

Beth was found by others and carried home. She was seriously injured and had to stay in bed for many weeks. At last she was able to be up, but deep scars showed where she had been beaten. Her back had also been injured and remained crooked for the rest of her life. But the joy she experienced in her soul more than made up for her crooked body and difficult life.

If the Holy Spirit works in your heart, then you, too, will receive strength to part with sinful pleasures; then you, too, will be drawn to the Lord Jesus and will learn to trust Him alone. You, too, will suffer persecution for Christ's sake. Only then will you learn to do His holy will out of love to Him.

Question: What did Joseph do when Potiphar's wife asked him to commit a sinful act?
Scripture reading: Genesis 39; 1 Samuel 20.

7. Bill's First Job

Mary Hudson was very thoughtful as she sat in her old rocking chair. Ten years had passed since her dear husband's death. Her son, Billy, was only five years old at the time he lost his father. Life had been very hard since that time. Mary had struggled to find ways of earning a living for herself and her little boy. But now she was becoming older, and she was not able to do as much as before.

"Please, Mother, you know you will have to let me go out to find work sooner or later. Please let me try to find a job in town. Winter is coming, and I want to help pay for what we need!"

"I know that is true, Bill. But I am worried. There is so much wickedness there. You have always lived quietly here in the country. How can you face the many temptations that are in town? Even though we would have to remain very poor, I pray that you will always remember to be honest. It is better to be poor than to do that which is not right. Yet, you should try to get work. If it must be in town, then always ask the Lord to show you what you must do."

Bill went to town and asked at many stores and businesses for a job. But times were hard and no one could afford to hire him. At last he found work in a drapery shop. He could work as a clerk if he was willing to do as Mr. Howe, his employer, asked. Bill was so thankful to have a job that he quickly agreed to do his best.

Mr. Howe was very kind to Bill and took time to train him himself. Bill worked hard and was very anxious to please his employer. He and his mother were both very thankful that he could help provide for their needs for the coming season.

As Bill's training continued, however, he began to wonder if everything he was asked to do was quite right. At first, he took for granted that everything Mr. Howe asked him to do was normal. When something seemed a bit strange to him, Bill would tell himself, "After all, Mr. Howe is an experienced business man, isn't he? Then this must be how business is done." But after working there for a while longer, Bill began to become very uncomfortable with what he was being trained to do.

Mrs. Smithers was known to be a very wealthy lady. When she came to the shop one day, Mr. Howe told Bill, "Look at this lady now. See how richly she is dressed? You can tell she has lots of money. When she asks for the price on anything, just double the usual price. She can afford to pay it!"

"But Mr. Howe, won't she know that's not true?" Bill hesitated.

"If she says anything, tell her that you're giving it to her for the wholesale price and that she won't find it any cheaper anywhere else." Laughing to himself, Mr. Howe left Bill at the counter to wait on Mrs. Smithers.

When Mrs. Smithers entered the store, Bill did his best to do as he was instructed. Mrs. Smithers bought what she needed, but she gave Bill a strange look. It was as though she noticed him hesitate when telling her the price. This bothered Bill, and he began more and more to think things through for himself.

Mrs. Ames was not quite as wealthy as Mrs. Smithers. When she came to the store, Bill was instructed to add an additional half of the price to the supplies. "You will soon learn to judge by how people dress and talk as to just how much you can get them to pay!" Bill was told. And Mr. Howe always stayed close enough to see how well Bill did. If ever Bill hesitated to raise the prices, Mr. Howe would give him trouble later.

Finally Bill could not keep quiet any longer. One day when no customers were in the store he said, "Mr. Howe, I'm not comfortable with changing the prices all the time. I'm sure it can't be right!"

"Now, Bill!" Mr. Howe laughed. "That's the way everyone does business. Why, I'm a faithful member of my church. I wouldn't do anything wrong!"

Bill was totally confused. "Maybe I just don't understand business," he thought. But that Sunday night in church, Bill heard Reverend Morris preach about what it meant to seek the Lord. The more Bill heard, the more sure he was that he was deceiving the people at the store. His mother's words also came back to him: "Bill, it is better to remain poor than to do that which is not right. Always remember to be honest!"

"But what must I do?" he argued with himself. "If I don't do what Mr. Howe asks, I'll lose my job. And Mother needs all the help I can give."

Rev. Morris was known to be very upright, and straightforward when he spoke. Bill decided to speak to the minister about his problem after the service. "At least I can be sure he will tell me what is right and what is not," he thought.

Rev. Morris welcomed Bill into his study. Soon Bill had told him how his mother had always warned him against sin and reminded him how important it was to be honest. He also explained what he was required to do for Mr. Howe. "And Mr. Howe is a church member," he concluded, "so now I don't know what to think anymore."

"Your mother is a much better guide than your employer!" exclaimed Rev. Morris. "No matter if Mr. Howe is a church member, he is teaching you to lie and to deceive people. Follow your mother's advice and refuse to raise any more prices!"

"But I will lose my job for sure."

"Lose it then! Don't hesitate for a minute! If he sends you away for being honest, then you will know for sure that he is a dishonest man!"

"But my mother will be so disappointed if I lose the first job I ever had! What will she think of me? She'll probably think I'm not yet fit to work after all." Bill said sadly.

"Not at all," Rev. Morris replied. "Just tell her the truth. She will be glad to know that you would rather lose a job than be dishonest."

Bill's eyes filled with tears and he couldn't speak. He saw what he had to do, but he was filled with concern. Finally he sobbed, "I realize now that I can't stay working there. But whatever can I do? I have tried so many places before. I don't know where to look for another place to work."

"Do you pray?" asked Rev. Morris.

"Yes, I do pray," said Bill, "but I still don't know what to do about a job."

Reverend Morris continued by telling Bill about those things which are most important. He urged him to trust the Lord for all things in his life. "Ask Him to guide you in looking for a job," he said. But he also explained that it was much more important to seek the Lord Jesus Christ as the only hope for salvation. Bill listened carefully and promised to visit again soon.

When Bill went to work the next morning, he almost lost his courage. But with a prayer in his heart, he spoke to Mr. Howe. "I can no longer lie to people about the prices, Mr. Howe, for that is what I have been doing all this time. Can't we just be honest with the customers?"

Bill lost his job just as he had feared. But word soon spread how he would rather not work than be dishonest. The result was remarkable. Bill soon had a better job and was given more responsibility and better pay, and within a few years, Mr. Howe lost his business and became very poor.

Bill continued to visit Rev. Morris, and the Lord used these visits to lead him to seek the Lord with his whole heart. He became a lost sinner before God, and was eventually brought by the work of the Holy Spirit and the grace of God to trust in Jesus Christ alone for salvation. The Lord Jesus revealed Himself to Bill as his own Savior who had died on the Cross for lost sinners.

After a few years, Bill was able to start his own business. He also joined Rev. Morris's church. Throughout his life Bill saw the blessings he received from listening to the advice of his God-fearing mother.

Question: What commandments did Bill break under the instructions of his employer? What happened when Bill obeyed God's commands?
Scripture reading: Proverbs 11:1-6.

8. Captain Barker's Trial

Many years ago James Barker became captain of a whaling ship. He had sailed with his crew for many years and was well-known. No one was more profane than he was. Every command he gave was punctuated with swear words.

Captain Barker was set to sail the Pacific Ocean on another long whaling hunt. But the night before he sailed he heard a sermon preached in his home town. This sermon left a deep impression on this careless captain. The Lord worked a great change in his heart.

The ship sailed the next day as planned. Before long, however, the crew noticed a difference in their captain. They soon noticed that he did not swear any more. Instead, Captain Barker seemed to have a reverent attitude. Often they saw his lips moving and realized that he was praying.

Captain Barker and his crew sailed for several weeks. They searched the endless waters, but no whales were to be seen. But one Sunday evening, just as the sun was setting, one of the crew cried out, "Look, over there! There's one!" Everyone immediately sprang into action. Captain

Barker was also excited at first. But the words, "Remember the Sabbath Day to keep it holy," (Exodus 20:8) sounded in his heart. The men were preparing to let the boats down to go after the whale. But suddenly Captain Barker shouted, "Men, wait! We will not be going after that whale today."

"You can't be serious," one man answered. "We've sailed for weeks already, and this is the first whale we've seen."

"Who will feed my wife and children if this whale gets away?" questioned another.

But Captain Barker remained firm. "I will personally pay for any loss you suffer from this," he quietly answered.

This helped settle down most of the men, but first mate Stoffer was not satisfied. Besides, he was next to the captain in rank and wanted to show his authority. "What about Mr. Peters, the owner of the ship?" he challenged. "Do you think he will be pleased with this loss?" Seeing a smile on the faces of several men he continued, "Sign a statement saying that this is your idea, but that we do not agree with you."

The captain realized that no ship owner would ever hire him as captain if he did such a thing. But he calmly answered, "It would not be legal to sign such a paper on Sunday, but I will do this for you tomorrow."

First mate Stoffer tried again. "Captain, I have a wife and five children to care for. If it is in God's providence to bring us a whale on Sunday, then we must catch it!"

But Captain Barker did not seem to hear what his first mate said. He dropped down onto a bench, completely lost in thought. Over and over he repeated the words, "Thy will be done."

Suddenly Stoffer shook his captain by the shoulder and cried, "Captain, look at how fast the barometer is falling! We are in for a storm! It's a good thing that none of our men went out in the boats."

Within half an hour every crew member was struggling against a fierce hurricane. All night vicious winds and waves battered the ship. But the brave seamen struggled on. Many began to pray to the Lord to save them. The Lord answered their prayers and protected them from all harm.

After three days the storm finally passed. But the crew found that they had been carried hundreds of miles in the wrong direction. They were in waters that had always been known as the poorest area for fishing. The men who had been filled with terror from the storm were now filled with despair. But as the sea calmed, their despair turned to joy. They found that they were surrounded by a large group of whales. Captain Barker bowed his head in wonder and thanksgiving. He thought of the words of the Lord Jesus, "Cast thy net on the right side of the ship, and ye shall find." (John 21:6) What an unexpected blessing they now received!

Within a very short time, the crew had

successfully captured two whales. The following days were very busy. They soon had as many whales as their ship could carry. The grateful captain and crew were able to return to their home port several months earlier than usual.

Mr. Peters was very surprised to see his ship sail into port so soon after leaving. Captain Barker greeted him as he and the crew came ashore. The crew gathered around the two men as their captain told Mr. Peters of all that had happened. "The Lord has delivered us from the storm. And He has blessed us greatly for obeying His command to honor the Sabbath Day," Captain Barker said as he ended his story.

"You have been wonderfully delivered and richly blessed!" exclaimed Mr. Peters. "It is entirely up to you in the future whether you let down the boats on Sunday or not."

By the grace of God, Captain Barker continued to obey his Master. For several years no other ships brought in as much theirs.

God moves in a mysterious way
His wonders to perform;
He sets His footsteps in the sea,
And rides upon the storm.

Question: Can you think of other Bible stories where people were delivered by God from fierce storms?
Scripture reading: John 12:23-26.

9. "I Can't Make up My Mind"

Robert was the oldest son of godly parents. Mr. and Mrs. Smith obeyed the command in Deuteronomy 6:7: "Thou shalt teach them diligently unto thy children, and shalt talk of them when thou sittest in thine house, and when thou walkest by the way, and when thou liest down, and when thou risest up."

Robert went to Sunday School every Sunday, and his teacher often told the children of the need to remember their Creator in the days of their youth. Robert always knew his lessons and could recite his Bible passages without any mistakes. He listened with interest to the teacher.

One very rainy Sunday, Robert was the only child who came to class. But his teacher was there and he took the opportunity to press home the truth upon Robert's conscience with more than usual earnestness. He talked to Robert about the promises of God and told him that twelve years were already wasted in Robert's young life. The teacher urged Robert to go to Jesus without delay to have his sins washed away and his heart renewed.

Mr. and Mrs. Smith noticed that Robert

was more quiet than usual that afternoon and throughout the week that followed. The next Sabbath, the teacher told the story of Jesus and the children, and again urged the children to go to the Savior, the only true refuge. The teacher saw that the Holy Spirit was striving with Robert, and talked to the children about the need to be born again.

Robert's parents prayed much, noticing that Robert struggled. After some time, Mr. Smith spoke with his son. He told Robert the danger of refusing to bow before God, and that he should flee to Him for salvation while he was young.

Robert sighed. "The last four weeks or so, I felt I wanted a new heart, Dad, but when I'd get home, I would put it off. Whenever I think about it, I just can't make up my mind."

Mr. Smith reminded him of the danger of grieving the Holy Spirit, warning him that this could be his last opportunity, and that Jesus was ready to forgive now.

"I know, Dad, I know," replied Robert, with tears in his eyes, "but I don't know if I'm ready to ask for a new heart now."

From that time on, Robert's seriousness grew less and less. The Spirit left him. Robert was "almost persuaded," like Felix, who "trembled, and answered, Go thy way for this time; when I have a convenient season, I will call for thee" (Acts 24:25), and like King Agrippa, who said, "Almost thou persuadest me to be a Christian" (Acts 26:28).

Children, it is a dangerous thing to resist the Spirit of God. When you have impressions or convictions, go to God and plead for mercy. Ask the Holy Spirit to continue working in you, and to make you His child.

"Cast me not away from thy presence; and take not thy holy spirit from me" (Ps. 51:11).

"As I live, saith the Lord GOD, I have no pleasure in the death of the wicked; but that the wicked turn from his way and live: turn ye, turn ye from your evil ways; for why will ye die, O house of Israel?" (Ezek. 33:11).

"Behold, I stand at the door, and knock: if any man hear my voice, and open the door, I will come in to him, and sup with him, and he with me" (Rev. 3:20). Lord, give me to hear Thy voice!

Question:Which religious leader did Jesus speak to one night about being born again? What advice are we given in 3 John 11? What is the danger in putting off praying for a new heart?
Scripture reading: Acts 24:1-27.

10. "Mine's a Religion for All Weather"

Along the Cornish Coast lay a village where the people were very poor. Many of them were fishermen. The year 1859 was a stormy one, and for nearly a month the men could not go out fishing because of the high winds.

At last, on a Sunday morning, the wind died down. It seemed to be a perfect day to go fishing. Several men met together early that morning.

"What do you think?" asked one of them. "We haven't been out in the fishing boats for almost a month now."

"If it weren't Sunday, I'd be on my boat right now," stated another man.

"I think it would be all right if we went fishing today. We are so poor and we need money badly," a third man said. "I'm going fishing. I know it's Sunday, but today it is necessary."

Before the fisherman could leave, another man joined the little group. "Wait!" he said kindly. "Don't tell me you are going to break God's law with your excuses!"

Several other villagers had gathered around them, but the man continued: "Mine's a religion for all weather—storm or calm weather. 'This is the love of God, that we keep His commandments.' (1 John 5:3) 'Remember the Sabbath day to keep it holy.' (Exodus 20:8) That's the law, my friends. Jesus came to fulfill the law, not to break it. True, we are poor and need money badly, but what does that matter? It's better to be poor and have God's smile than to be rich and have God's frown. Go fishing if you dare, but I never knew of any good that came of a religion that changed with the wind."

The fishermen listened to the wise words of their friend. They all went home and dressed for church. The day was spent worshipping God.

In the evening, just when the boats would have been heading home had they gone out, a sudden storm arose. It raged terribly for two days. After that came several days of calm weather. During that time the men caught so many fish that there was no more complaining in the village, for God had supplied their needs. This is truly a religion for all weather. Those who have saving faith desire to serve God at all times.

Question: How many days has God given us to do our work in? What has God done to the Sabbath day?
Scripture reading: Exodus 16:13-31, Exodus 20:11.

11. Quenching the Spirit

There was once a minister God used during a time of revival. This minister also taught some courses at a local college, and many students in his class were born again. One young man in the class was intelligent, pleasant and well-liked. He attended the services at the college almost every evening, and came under conviction of sin. The minister prayed continually for this young man's conversion, and felt he could be used in God's kingdom. Often the two would talk about the need to be born again. The minister felt that something hindered the young man and wondered just what it could be.

One evening, the young man came to visit the minister. "I am grateful for all the time you have spent with me and have come to tell you that I've made up my mind, but in a different way than you expected."

The minister waited, puzzled as to what the young man meant.

"I've decided not to become a Christian just yet," explained the young man. "You see, I have always wanted to go into politics, but I believe that I will never succeed if I become a Christian. So I have decided to pursue a career in politics, and put Christianity on hold for now."

The minister was devastated. With tears streaming down his face, he pleaded with the young man not to do this. He knew how dangerous it was to put off seeking the Lord. But the young man's mind was made up. He had made his choice, and was determined to stick to it.

So the young man entered political life. He was very successful. But what was his end? Did he seek the Lord at the end of his life? Did he become a Christian? No, this promising young man died without the Lord and entered eternity without Christ's redeeming blood.

Never put off seeking the Lord. Never shake off the strivings of the Holy Spirit. When the apostle Paul preached to Felix, Felix did the same thing this young man did. He "trembled, and answered, Go thy way for this time; when I have a convenient season, I will call for thee" (Acts 24:25b). King Agrippa had the same response: "Almost thou persuadest me to be a Christian" (Acts 26:28). Flee to the Lord Jesus for mercy. Do not rest until you are redeemed by the blood of the Savior.

Question: Have you asked the Lord to save you and to keep you safe by His grace? What happened to the young man who postponed fleeing to God for salvation? Scripture reading: Hebrews 2:1-4.

12. Raymond Jones

Raymond Jones was twelve years old. He was looking forward to the summer vacation because his father had promised to ask the farmers he knew if Raymond could spend the summer on the farm. Raymond was thrilled. He loved farms and animals, and was eager to learn about caring for the animals and the crops.

Mr. Jones spoke to Mr. Jenkins, who sold the Jones's butter and milk. He said he'd be happy to have some help on the farm.

As soon as school was out, Raymond packed his suitcase. Bright and early the following morning, he said goodbye to his mother, and his father took him to the Jenkins farm. A quick hug from his father, some last words of farewell, and Raymond was ready to start his summer job.

Raymond helped with the chores each morning and evening. He helped make butter and cleaned the milk pails. He worked in the garden and sometimes helped Mr. Jenkins in the fields. Because Raymond was still young, and Mr. Jenkins didn't want to work him too hard, Raymond was allowed some free time every afternoon. Raymond enjoyed farm life immensely.

But one thing bothered him terribly. Mr. Jenkins swore often. Raymond didn't like that at all. It made him uncomfortable. After a few days, Raymond made a decision.

"Mr. Jenkins, I'd like to go home, please."

Mr. Jenkins was surprised. "What's wrong? Are you homesick?"

"No sir," answered Raymond.

"Don't you like it here? I thought you were enjoying yourself."

"I love it here," answered Raymond. He took a deep breath. "But I am troubled by your swearing sir. It hurts my feelings because I love the God whose name you are taking in vain. I'll have to go home."

Mr. Jenkins was silent. Raymond's words had a great effect on him. He knew how much Raymond loved the farm. He admired Raymond's courage and felt ashamed of himself. After a few moments, Mr. Jenkins spoke. "I'll tell you what, Raymond. You stay here on the farm and I'll quit swearing."

Raymond's face broke into a happy smile. "Really? That's great! I'm so glad! Thank you!"

Raymond stayed for the entire summer vacation, and Mr. Jenkins kept his promise. He never swore again.

Question: Why did it bother Raymond to hear Mr. Jenkins swear?
Scripture readings: Exodus 20:7; Leviticus 19:12; Matthew 5:34; James 3:10, 5:12.

13. Satisfied with the Best

A New York business man was riding a Fourth Avenue trolley car one day, when he heard someone call out, "Wait! Mr. Conductor, please stop the car! I can't run very fast!"

The trolley car stopped, and a crippled boy hobbled up the steps. He was about twelve years old, and the business man could tell by his clothing that he came from a wealthy family. Yet his face was lined with suffering and pain. However, the boy was bright and cheerful and as he sat down on a bench, he put his crutch behind him on the floor and placed his crippled leg in a more comfortable position. Then he smiled at the people around him.

At the next stop, the person next to the boy got off, and the business man went to sit beside him. He heard the boy humming "Rock of Ages" softly to himself.

"That's one of my favorite hymns," commented the business man.

"It helps to sing when my leg hurts," answered the boy.

"Does it hurt often?" asked the man kindly.

"Yes. I was born like this. The doctor says it will always be like this."

"Well, my dear boy," said the business man, "under these circumstances, how can you be so happy and cheerful?"

The boy smiled. "Jesus, my Savior, has sent this trial for me to bear. My father tells me that God would not have sent it unless He knew it would be best for me. And I think I should be satisfied with the best?"

This touched the man's heart. He shook the boy's hand. "Thank you for the lesson you have taught me today," he said. "I'll never forget it as long as I live."

The boy only smiled shyly in return.

Sometimes we think everything should go smoothly for us, don't we? When the Holy Spirit shows us that we are sinners, however, we see that we don't deserve God's blessings. Ask the Lord to give you a clean heart. Ask Him to wash away your sin, and to give you a love for God. Ask Him to make you thankful for His blessings, and to help you trust Him in all things.

"Thou wilt keep him in perfect peace, whose mind is stayed on thee: because he trusteth in thee. Trust ye in the LORD for ever: for in the LORD JEHOVAH is everlasting strength." (Isaiah 26:3-4).

Question: What do you do when God places difficulties and trials in your path? Do you complain and get angry? How does God want us to respond?
Scripture readings: Deuteronomy 8:2; Acts 16:16-34.

14. Saying "Please" and "Thank You"

Benny was a boy of about eight years of age. His father was not a Christian, but his mother did her best to teach Benny about God and His Word. Mealtimes did not include prayers or Bible reading; Benny's father refused to give God any respect in his home.

"Dad," began Benny one day, "Mom says that God made you. Did He, Dad?"

"Well, yes, He made me, I suppose."

"But aren't you glad He made you?" persisted Benny.

"Of course I am, Benny! Why do you ask such strange questions?"

Benny was trying to figure out some things which he did not understand. Not long after this, Benny went to visit his Uncle Sam. This man was a true Christian. He always asked a blessing at their meals, and had family devotions every day. Benny was very impressed by all this, and he wondered why his father did not allow this in his home.

When Benny was seated at the breakfast table after he had returned home, he asked, "Daddy, why does Uncle Sam ask for God's blessing at mealtimes?"

"I guess it's because he wants to," answered Benny's father.

Benny smiled proudly at his father. "Uncle Sam told me he wants to thank God for his food, but I told him you worked for your food. God doesn't give it to you, does He?"

Benny's father sighed. "Well," he said slowly, "to be honest, God does give us our food."

Benny looked up in astonishment. He hadn't expected his father to say this. For a while he ate in silence. Then he looked at his father and asked another question. "Daddy, does God want you to thank Him, too?"

Benny's father rubbed his hands over his face, and answered quietly, "Yes, son, I suppose He does."

Benny was quiet again as he thought about this. Then, with a very serious expression on his face, he said, "Dad, I'm glad that God is not like you. We'd never get anything more to eat, and then we'd starve."

"What do you mean by that?"

"I was just thinking," explained Benny, "that you wouldn't let Becky have that apple the other day because she wouldn't say 'please,' and if God was that way, He would never give us anything more, because we don't thank Him, like Uncle Sam does, or say 'please.'"

"Benny," growled his father, "that's enough! I'm tired of all your questions!" Angrily he left the room, going to work without saying "good-bye."

Benny's father went to his office and tried to focus on his work. But he could not forget what his son had said. He began to see that he was very wrong in not thanking God for His many mercies. Putting aside his papers, and closing his office door, Benny's father spent some time thinking and praying.

To the surprise of his entire family, when they sat down to eat that evening, Benny's father said "please." He thanked God for their food, and asked His blessing upon it. He asked his wife and children for their forgiveness in not teaching them about God. He promised to do his best in honoring God and His Word in their home, and asked for their prayers for God to help him be a better father.

"If my people, which are called by my name, shall humble themselves, and pray, and seek my face, and turn from their wicked ways; then will I hear from heaven, and will forgive their sin, and will heal their land" (2 Chronicles. 7:14).

Question: Can you make a list of mercies that God has already given you in the hours since you got up this morning?
Scripture reading: John 6:1-14.

15. The Blessing of Prayer

The month of November arrived. The trees, which but a short while ago were arrayed in their splendid autumn dress, were now bare, and the chilly wind whistled through the branches.

In the village of Alden stood a beautiful mansion. A well-to-do family lived there, but with the arrival of the winter season, they moved to the city for the long, gray months.

While they were gone, various tradesmen would come to do repair work. An old gardener was given responsibility for caring for the place. He lived with his wife in a small, tidy house some distance from the mansion.

The winter season also brought a change in the lives of the gardener and his wife. While the family who lived in the mansion was engaged in worldly amusements, the gardener and his wife enjoyed the winter months for very different reasons. Often God's people would come together in their small home for prayer, singing and godly conversations. Some would come from long distances and stay for several days.

Early in December, two young men from a neighboring town arrived at the gate of the mansion. It was still early in the morning and they carried their painting equipment with them.

"Oh," the gardener thought, "they must be the painters who have to repaint some of the rooms in the mansion."

They seemed to be two happy, lively young men, and their motto seemed to be: "Enjoy life while you can!" From early morning until evening they sang as they worked. These songs were not, however, to the honor of God. But what else could you expect? A person whose heart has not been renewed by the Holy Spirit enjoys the things of this life, and youth is the time in which the world offers the most temptations. They did not think of the Scripture which says, "Rejoice, oh young man, in thy youth; and let thy heart cheer thee in the days of thy youth, and walk in the ways of thine heart, and in the sight of thine eyes: but know thou, that for all these things God will bring thee in to judgment" (Ecclesiastes 11:9). They did not seriously consider the Judge who judges righteously and before whom they would have to appear one day to give an account.

This became very clear when noontime arrived. When the sun had reached its highest point and the clock in the large home struck twelve, the work was interrupted for a while in order to eat the bread which the men had brought for lunch. But even while they were having lunch, the

Creator and Giver of all good things was not remembered. They ate their bread without prayer.

This first lunch, however, did not go unnoticed by the gardener's wife. Sitting in front of her window, she could look right into the room where the painters were working.

"Oh, these boys," she thought. "They are in the springtime of their lives, and they spend their best strength in the service of Satan. They are estranged from the living God. Oh I hope that they might learn to seek the God that made them, in uprightness of heart!"

She went on with her work, but her thoughts wandered to these two young men. "Am I being faithful to my God if I let them continue on in the way of destruction without warning them?" she asked herself. "Is it not my calling to point them to the new birth and the renewing of the heart which is so necessary for eternity? Don't I have an opportunity now and don't I have to 'sow beside all waters'?"

Suddenly she thought of a way to direct the painters to the only way of salvation.

She waited until the next lunch hour, and then she approached them. "It seems like you are eating your lunch without a hot drink," she observed. "Come with me to my house where it is warm. I'll gladly make you some coffee."

They gladly accepted the invitation. As

soon as the steaming coffee was poured for them, the painters wanted to begin eating, without praying. The gardener's wife, however, said, "Yesterday I noticed that you did not ask God for a blessing for the good gifts that He has given you. You probably never do that, so I will ask a blessing for you."

She did not ask for an answer and prayed in touching and simple language. She especially prayed for the conversion of the two painters. During the meal she told how much blessedness there is to be enjoyed in the service of the Lord in contrast with the wretchedness of the service of the world.

What the painters were thinking during all of this we do not know, but the expression on their faces showed that they were not enjoying this kind of talk at all, much less the prayer. In spite of this, the woman closed the meal with a prayer of thanksgiving. Then she invited them to come again the following day.

As soon as the men were out of the house, they said to one another, "That lady is kind enough, but her talk about religion makes me sick. We shouldn't go there anymore."

"Yes, her coffee is good, but her prayers are a pain to listen to. She must think that we are criminals, judging by her prayers!"

The next day, the temptation of the delicious hot coffee got the better of them, and they decided to go anyway and ignore the woman's religious talk. From then on, they kept coming until their work was completed. Then they joked with each other that they were rid of her pious praying.

The gardener's wife wondered if her prayer would bear fruit. She knew she did not need to worry about that. She had done her duty, and had not been ashamed of the gospel of Christ. She must leave the outcome to the Lord.

A few years passed by quickly. It was winter again, and the snow fell softly, covering the frozen ground with a thick, white blanket.

The gardener's wife sat near the fireplace. Occasionally she looked out at the beautiful snow. It made her think of Psalm 147:16, "He giveth snow like wool." She admired God's power in nature, but little did she think that soon she would also see His power displayed in the realm of grace.

Due to the snow, she did not hear the two men approaching until they stood at the door. The gardener's wife did not know who they were, but when one asked if they could stay for a while, she recognized the voice and remembered the two painters, who, some years ago, were her daily guests. She looked at them in surprise. One of the men said, "This time we're not here for your coffee, but we'd like to tell you what the Lord has done for our souls."

Soon they were gathered around the fire,

and the painters related what they had experienced during those last few years.

The serious prayers of the woman had been engraved on their consciences, and they became more and more alarmed at the thought of having to appear before God. The Lord showed them that the woman was speaking the truth. They felt that they could not stand before Him on the Judgment Day.

No more vain songs were heard while they were working, but many times silent tears ran down their cheeks while this prayer arose from their hearts: "Be merciful, oh God, be merciful to me!"

The same young men, who never used to pray, now became secret wrestlers at the throne of grace. They pleaded for the salvation of their souls. It could be said of them what the Lord said of Saul: "Behold, he prayeth!" (Acts 9:11)

There was one very special and unforgettable moment in which the two friends became brothers. They were painting one day when one asked the other, "Why are you so quiet?"

The other answered, "Why are *you* so quiet?"

The first one, though hesitantly, poured out his heart to the other, and told his companion that the prayer of the gardener's wife burned in his heart as fire. It condemned him, and he felt he was a sinner before God. He pleaded for mercy and desired to be washed in the blood of the Lamb. Then the other told him he was feeling the same way.

It is easier to sense than to describe what those two men felt. Sweet ties of brotherhood were formed, and even though they did not know these words at that time, they experienced: "How good and how pleasant it is for brethren to dwell together in unity!" (Psalm 133:1).

That evening, in the gardener's home, the same thing was experienced. Together they praised the Lord whose ways are past finding out and whose mercy endures forever. They realized that "the effectual fervent prayer of a righteous man availeth much." (James 5:16).

The God-fearing gardener and his wife have long since entered into that rest which remains to God's people. We don't know if the painters are still alive, but if we would ever meet them before the throne of the Lamb, we will also have to have of that heart-renewing work of the Holy Spirit.

Question: In Luke 22:17 who else thanked God for their food?
Scripture reading: Matthew 6:5-15.

16. The Little Fishing Spot

The fishing boats sail through the canal. They are on their way to the old fishing grounds. The fishermen are all hoping for a good catch. Skipper Arie Blaak and his nephew Martin are near the end of the line. Their little boat cannot go very fast.

Skipper Blaak thinks back to the time when, years ago, he almost drowned. But God spared his life. He was saved in a wonderful way. The Lord blessed this experience to the skipper's soul. He learned to see himself as a lost sinner. The Lord showed mercy and heard his cries. Since then the Lord often encouraged and comforted Arie.

Skipper Blaak and Martin sailed out of the canal into the open waters. All the fishermen knew where the good fishing spots were, and these were already taken. Skipper Blaak was disappointed. Only one small spot was left. They could only set up half their nets there. Besides, everyone knew that no fish were ever caught there. Because of the sand bar, the fishing boat could not come near the little fishing spot. They would have to use the rowboat.

Skipper Blaak hesitated, "Let's try it, Martin," he said. "If the Lord will grant His blessing we will catch some fish."

Martin nodded. A silent prayer arose from the skipper's heart. Everything was possible with God. If they didn't try, they wouldn't catch any fish, but if the Lord helped them, they would catch fish to sell at the market. Skipper Blaak and Martin both thought of the Lord Jesus who told His disciples to cast their nets on the other side of the boat. Then they had so many fish that they needed another boat to get them to shore.

Martin dropped the anchor. He put half of the nets into the rowboat. The men quickly set up their poles and arranged the nets. The other fishermen shrugged their shoulders and shook their heads. "Nobody's ever caught anything there that I can remember," said an old fisherman. "Blaak's wasting his time."

Before long everything was ready. "Let's hope for a blessing, Martin," sighed Skipper Blaak.

Together they entered the little cabin in the fishing boat. They ate their lunch in silence. Each was occupied with his own thoughts.

"We'll wait until low tide, Martin," instructed Uncle Arie. "It's not very easy to walk there. Too many holes."

At low tide they rowed toward their nets. At the sand bar, the men got out and walked through the shallow water. An amazing sight greeted them. Their nets were full of fish!

"I don't think I've ever caught so many fish at once!" The skipper's eyes were damp with tears. "Quick, Martin! Get the rowboat!"

Martin pulled the rowboat as near to the nets as possible. Bushels of fish were loaded into the rowboat. The little rowboat could not hold many fish, and the men made several trips to the fishing vessel to empty the rowboat.

Finally they were finished. The men looked at the hundreds of fish they caught. "The Lord has done this, Martin. He is still the same Master of the Universe who helped the disciples catch their great catch." The skipper wipeed his eyes with his handkerchief. "God is so good and merciful."

At last they were ready to sail for the harbor. They had a heavy load. The other fishermen were amazed to see such a big catch.

Skipper Blaak was very glad to be able to show his wife and children the many fish the Lord gave them. They had many reasons to be thankful. The Lord had richly blessed them. He hears the needy when they cry.

Question: Read 1 Kings 17. Which people are provided with food in this chapter? Scripture reading: John 21:1-14.

17. The Swiss Farmer and the Lord's Day

In the fertile valley of Emmenthal, in Switzerland, lived a young farmer. Golden grain swayed in his large field, ready for harvest. On a Sunday afternoon, the farmer noticed dark clouds gathering on the mountain tops, and the nearby mountain stream swelling in its banks. He quickly called his farmhands together.

"I want you to get as much of this grain in the barn as you can before the storm strikes. If you can manage to put a thousand sheaves away, I'll pay you extra."

The men nodded and began to move toward the barn to get their scythes, but they were stopped by an old woman's voice. They turned and saw their boss's grandmother hobbling towards them with the help of two crutches. She was a kind lady, about eighty years old. God had made her one of His children and she had great respect for Him and His commandments.

"John, John," she said with tears in her eyes. "As long as I can remember, I have never seen an ear of corn harvested on the Lord's Day, and yet we have always been loaded with blessings and never come short. So far the year has been very dry, so what harm can a little rain do? Besides, God who gives the rain gives the grain as well, and we must receive things as God sends them. John, do not desecrate this holy day!"

By this time the farmhands had gathered around John and his grandmother. Some older men understood the wisdom of her advice, but many of the younger hands laughed and said to each other, "That's old-fashioned! Times have changed."

"Grandma," said John, "all new things must have a beginning. I really don't see anything wrong with this. God doesn't care if we spend the day sleeping or working. I think He'll be glad to see the grain safely in the barn, rather than rotting in the fields. And what if it rains all week?"

"My dear young man," persisted his grandmother, "all things are in God's hands. You know I am your grandmother. I ask you, in God's Name, not to work today. I would rather eat no bread for a whole year, than abuse the Lord's Day."

"Oh, Grandma!" exclaimed John, throwing up his hands in exasperation. He felt foolish being reprimanded before his employees. "If I do it this once, it doesn't mean I'm in the habit of doing it. Besides, it's a sin not to save my crop!"

"But, John, God's commandments are always the same. And what will it profit you to have all the grain in your barn, if you lose your soul?"

John was beginning to feel annoyed.

"Don't you worry about me!" he laughed uncomfortably. "Okay guys, let's get the grain in before we lose it! Rain doesn't wait for anyone!"

So saying, he rudely turned his back on his grandmother. She watched in silence as he ran toward the stable to hitch the horses to the wagon. Tearfully, she committed him to the throne of God's grace, pleading for mercy on behalf of her grandson.

The men worked furiously, glancing occasionally at the ever-darkening sky. When the last sheaf of grain was put in the barn, and the first drop of rain fell, the men wiped their damp brows, congratulating one another. John was more jovial than the others. With an air of triumph he said to his grandmother, "Well, it's safe in the barn now. Now it can rain as hard and as long as it wants to! No storm can get at my grain now!"

The old woman sighed and shook her head sadly, "You are forgetting one thing, John. Above your roof is God's roof."

Suddenly the sky was oddly lit. A moment's silence followed, and then a deafening clap of thunder. Fear and alarm showed on everyone's face.

"Oh!" gasped the first one who could find his voice. "The barn! It's on fire!"

The men rushed out of the house. The barn, which held the grain of the entire afternoon's labors, was ablaze. Through the flames and smoke they could catch glimpses of the once golden grain now smoldering in the intense heat.

The farmhands who had been so proud of their success stood helplessly by as John's harvest was devoured by fire. Only the aged grandmother seemed composed. She prayed and whispered continually, "'What shall it profit a man if he gain the whole world and lose his own soul?'" (Matthew 16:26) Oh, heavenly Father, let thy will, and not ours, be done!"

It was not long before the barn was completely destroyed. Nothing was saved. John had said his harvest was safely under his roof, but he learned that God's roof was over his roof. Indeed, "all things are under His feet" (Hebrews 2:8).

Question: Do God's commands change? What is the difference between worldly possessions and your soul (see Matthew 6:19-20)? In Zephaniah 2:12-13, what happened to those people who did not believe in God?
Scripture reading: 1 Kings 22.

18. Theo's Question

Theo ran round the room, pulling his toy train and calling out. "Toot! Toot! All aboard!"

"Shh! Theo, Grandma has a bad headache today," chided Aunt Marie.

"Oh, I forgot," said Theo, covering his mouth with his hand. "I'll be very quiet," he promised.

For a few moments he whispered to himself as he played, but soon he was talking out loud again, "Toot, toot! Aunt Marie, do you want a ride?"

Aunt Marie looked up from the book she was reading. "Did you say something, Theo?"

"Do you want a ride on my train?" repeated Theo. "We're going to the zoo."

"No, Theo, not today," smiled his aunt.

"Why not?" asked the little boy. "If I had a real train that you could really sit in, would you go along then?"

"No, I still wouldn't go, at least not today. Tomorrow I might, though."

"But why not today?" questioned Theo.

"What day is it today, Theo?" asked Aunt Marie, laying aside the book she had been reading.

Theo thought for a moment. "Sunday."

"Right," answered his aunt, "and because it is Sunday, I wouldn't ride in your train."

Theo was amazed, "Why not?"

Aunt Marie thought for a while. She also asked God to give her the wisdom to teach this little boy the difference between Sunday and the other days of the week. She saw in Theo the sad result of her brother's choice to go his own way. She also realized that her nephew, although he was only six years old, had a never-dying soul.

Aunt Marie answered Theo's question carefully. "We were not given Sundays to do whatever we like. Sunday is the Lord's Day. It really belongs to the Lord. We should go to church and read good books on Sunday."

Theo was busy hooking up more cars behind the locomotive. "Who said that?" he asked.

"The Lord tells us that in His Book. The Bible is the Word of God," replied Aunt Marie.

"Does that Book tell us other things, too?" asked Theo, tugging at his train.

"Yes, it does. There are many nice stories in the Bible, too."

When his aunt mentioned stories, Theo looked up. "Do you know any of them? I like stories. Last night Mommy read about Tom Thumb."

"But the Bible doesn't have those kinds of stories in it. Come, sit beside me, and I'll tell you one."

Theo left his train, and climbed on the couch beside his aunt. "What's it about?"

"It's about a boy who was sold, and taken to a strange land, very far away from his dear father," informed Aunt Marie.

"Oh!" said Theo, his face suddenly serious.

Aunt Marie drew him close to her, and began the story of Joseph: "Far away, there is a land where it is always warm. In this country, there lived a man whose name was Jacob."

It was clear that Theo had never heard the story before. He interrupted so many times, and asked so many questions! But Aunt Marie did not mind at all. She went on with her story. She told Theo that no matter what Joseph's brothers did to him, the Lord protected him. The Lord cared for Joseph wherever he went. They could not have killed him for the Lord watched over him.

Theo asked, "Does the Lord live in Canaan or in Egypt?"

"This Lord is God, Theo, and He is all over. He was in Egypt and heard Joseph's prayers, and at the same time He was in Canaan and heard Jacob's prayers."

"That can't be," decided Theo.

"If the Lord were a man, then it couldn't be; but He is God, and He doesn't have a body like we have," explained Aunt Marie. "We can only be in one place at a time, but the Lord is in all places. He hears and sees us all the time. He even knows what we are thinking."

Theo was very puzzled. "How can that be? I never saw the Lord. Where is He?"

"We can't see Him, but one day everyone will see Him."

"When will that be?" Theo wanted to know.

"The Lord didn't tell us that. This is hard for you to understand, isn't it, Theo?" When he nodded, she said, "Ask the Lord to help you understand and believe it."

"Daddy never told me about this," remarked Theo. Then he suddenly burst out, "I don't believe it. How can the Lord be alive if I can't even see Him?"

For a moment Aunt Marie looked at Theo thoughtfully, silently begging God for His assistance. Then she said, "Theo, do you have an Uncle Ben?"

"Yes!" exclaimed Theo, brightening.

"Where does he live?"

"In Rio Grande," answered Theo, stumbling a little over the name.

"That's a strange name," commented his aunt. "Is that far away?"

"Uh-huh," replied Theo, forgetting his manners in his excitement. "Daddy says it's on the other side of a big, huge ocean."

"I've never seen your Uncle Ben. I've never been in that city where you say he lives. I don't believe you have an Uncle Ben!"

Theo jumped off the couch, and stood in front of his aunt. "Yes I do! It's true, really it is!"

"Well," continued Aunt Marie, "have you ever seen him or been to his house?"

"No, but Daddy and Mommy have told me about him lots of times."

Aunt Marie said quietly, "Oh, but you told me that your Mom and Dad tell you fairy tales sometimes. How do you know that this isn't just a fairy tale?"

"It's not a fairy tale!" Theo's eyes flashed. "He gave me a boat for my birthday, and my sister got a doll for hers."

"So you believe that you have an uncle just because some toys came in the mail? You've never seen him before."

"Well, Mommy and Daddy said I have an Uncle Ben," repeated Theo.

"Now, Theo, I want you to listen very carefully," said Aunt Marie, lifting him onto the couch again. "You say you've never seen your uncle, but he sends you letters and toys. That's how you know he lives in Rio Grande, right?"

Theo nodded.

"We've never seen the Lord either," continued Aunt Marie, "but we see His gifts every day and that's how we know He's alive right now. Just like you got a boat from Uncle Ben, so the Lord gives us food and drink and health every day. He gives us everything we need."

"Mommy gives me my food," objected Theo.

"What kind of food does your mother give you?" asked Aunt Marie.

"Bread and milk and potatoes and vegetables," listed Theo.

"Wait a minute," cut in Aunt Marie. "Where does your mother get the bread?"

"From the store," stated Theo.

"And where does the store manager get the bread?"

Theo didn't know.

"Bread is made from flour," explained Aunt Marie. "Flour is made from wheat. The farmers harvest the wheat with their tractors and equipment. How did that wheat get in the fields?"

"It grew there," answered Theo.

"Right," said Aunt Marie. "But who makes the wheat grow? The farmer?"

Theo shook his head.

"The Lord, whom you and I have never seen, makes the wheat and the vegetables and the potatoes grow so that we may have food to eat," explained Theo's aunt. "He also takes care of the cows that give us milk, and the chickens that give us eggs. If God would let all the plants and animals die, not one man could make them alive again, and very soon we would die too because we wouldn't have any food to eat. So," concluded Aunt Marie, "all those people who won't believe that there is a God in heaven are very foolish. Without God nothing could grow and we couldn't live either."

Theo listened quietly, his face very serious. Suddenly he said, "Then it's true that God is alive, isn't it, just like my Uncle Ben is alive, right?"

"Yes, Theo, that's right." Aunt Marie thanked the Lord for helping her to explain these things to her nephew. She wanted to impress upon him the need for a new heart. "You must ask the Lord often to forgive your sins and to make you His child, Theo. Only then will you be really happy." In the days and years ahead, Aunt Marie often made Theo's salvation a matter of prayer.

Theo visited his aunt often, and when he came home he would tell his parents what Aunt Marie had told him. At first they resented this, and for a while they refused to let Theo visit her, but he begged them to let him go, so at last they gave in. Although Theo's parents never went back to church, the Lord was pleased to use Aunt Marie's simple instructions to the salvation of her nephew and to set him in the right way.

Question: Think about other things that yu use every day. Aunt Marie explained to Theo how it was actually God who gave him the food that his mother made for him. Discuss how God has brought these other things into your life in a similar way.
Scripture reading: 2 Chronicles 24.

19. William Stands Firm

William and Elsie Anderson lived in a comfortable home with their six children. William was a mechanical engineer in a local factory. He earned very good wages.

William and Elsie were Christians who loved to serve the Lord. Their oldest son was studying for the ministry. The other children were attending school. The family felt loved and secure under the Christian guidance of their parents. William was a highly respected elder in the church that the family faithfully attended. The Andersons kept Sunday as a day belonging to God. The family attended church twice and observed the remaining hours with Bible study, singing, and prayer.

One Saturday William returned home from work very late. He came home too late to read the Bible and pray with his family before the children had gone to bed. Elsie was still sitting by the fire waiting for him. William told her about the problems that had arisen at work that day. "One of the main pieces of machinery broke down today," he explained. "Mr. Peters, our manager, ordered everyone to remain at work tonight, and to continue working tomorrow, on Sunday, too. He wants us to repair the machine and catch up with our work so that we will be back on schedule by Monday."

"But William!" Elsie exclaimed. "Mr. Peters has never asked any of his men to work on Sunday before! What did you tell him?"

William was quiet as he remembered how he had had to stand alone. At last he answered slowly, "None of the others protested, but I told him that I would work until midnight, but that I would not break God's command by working on Sunday. I think the others were laughing at me."

Elsie did her best to cheer him up. "Of course you did the right thing, William. How can Mr. Peters expect the Lord's blessing on his business if he orders his men to work on the Lord's Day?"

As the two continued talking quietly, they were suddenly surprised to hear the doorbell ring. It was past midnight, long past the time when they would expect anyone to come for a visit. William quickly arose to open the door. There stood a messenger from the factory. He had a message for William from Mr. Peters. "You are to come back to the factory immediately, William. If you don't come to help find the problem, we will never be able to fix that machine. And Mr. Peters warns you, that if you don't come, he will fire you immediately!"

William was surprised and angry. "I have

already explained to Mr. Peters why I will not work on Sunday. I refuse to do that which my conscience tells me is wrong. He thinks I will work anyway for fear of losing my job. Well, tell Mr. Peters that I will not break God's law for any earthly master, but will obey my Master in heaven. I cannot come in at all today."

William hardly had time to explain or reflect upon what had just happened when they heard an urgent knock on their door. Mr. Peters himself stood at the door, and it was plain to see that he was very upset. "Look here, Anderson," he said, "you simply have to come back! We can't possibly do the job without your help. You are the only one who understands how that machine works. If you don't come, it will be necessary for me to hire someone from another city, and that would be very costly."

"I'm sorry, Mr. Peters. I've already told you how I feel."

"You're not being reasonable, William. Listen, I'll give you a good raise in pay if you come now."

But William would not be persuaded. He had only one answer. "Mr. Peters, every hour of the Lord's Day belongs to the Lord. I will not work for you today. I am willing, however, to start at one o'clock Monday morning, but I will not work at all today."

When Mr. Peters saw that he could not change William's mind with threats or promises, he became very angry. "Mr.

Anderson," he stormed, "you are a fool! You are fired and will never work for me again!" With that, he left in haste.

William and Elsie sat down in shock. They began to realize what losing this job meant for their family. The Lord had blessed them with a comfortable living and they had no worries about the future. But suddenly they were faced with an impossible situation. Elsie tried hard to be brave. She had listened quietly to all that had been said, but now she sobbed as she tried to comfort her husband. Together they knelt in prayer and asked the Lord to care for them and their children. After casting their cares upon the Lord, they were able to lie down and sleep.

Both parents tried to keep Sunday as normally as possible. They sang the usual songs of praise with their children, and attended church with them. They never spoke about business matters or concerns on Sundays. This Sunday was no different. Their children didn't even realize that there was a problem. Even though William and Elsie expected a time of trial, they were able to place their burdens before God with the petition, "Thy will be done."

As the family lay peacefully sleeping, just after one o'clock Monday morning, a loud knock at the door startled them awake. William opened the door only to find his manager standing there again. This time, however, Mr. Peters was in a very different mood. He humbly apologized for speaking so harshly to William before and said, "Mr. Anderson, would you please consider coming to help us now that Sunday is past? We all apologize for how we treated you and promise that you will never be asked again to work on Sunday. We have tried and tried to fix that machine without you, but you can't believe how many problems we have had! I finally sent all the men home until I could speak to you again. Please come right away to help us out."

With gladness in his heart, William quickly dressed and went with his manager. He soon found the problem with the machine and had it back in working order in a short time. Mr. Peters and the others were very thankful for his help and sorry for their earlier treatment of him. How thankful William and Elsie were to see the faithfulness of God to them! What a beautiful lesson they could give their children the next day! They told them about the trial that had come and about how their father lost his job for refusing to break God's command. But they especially told them how the Lord had heard their prayer and gave his job back again.

Question: Look up the following Scripture to find out the names of two other people who praised God in the middle of very difficult circumstances: Acts 16:25.
Scripture reading: Daniel 1:1-21.

20. A Remarkable Deliverance

Mr. Burchell was pleased. After many hours of intense work, he had completed his first piece of cloth on the large weaving looms that stood in his attic. He had brought the cloth to a fabric shop in Bristol. The manager had examined it carefully.

"You do nice work, Mr. Burchell. We'll send you the money after we've sold your cloth. That usually takes a month or so."

That had been last week. Now he was visiting his friend, Mr. Williams. In the course of conversation Mr. Williams mentioned the very same fabric shop where Mr. Burchell had brought his cloth. He said it was most likely going bankrupt soon. Mr. Burchell, of course, was concerned about his piece of cloth. He had worked hard on all forty yards of that piece, and he was not about to see it taken from him without being paid for it. He immediately went to his boss and asked permission to be absent from work the next day. It was still early in the evening, and he figured he could be well on his way by nightfall.

He gathered a few items together and set off at a brisk pace. He had thirty miles to go, and he wanted to cover that distance by early morning.

When it was quite dark, he stopped at an inn along the way. At daybreak he was up and ready to continue.

The innkeeper asked him where he was off to.

"I'm headed for Bristol, sir," explained Mr. Burchell.

"Oh, then you should take the road to the Severn River. You'll be sure to find a boat there that'll take you down to Bristol in good time."

"Thank you for the tip, sir."

He took the road the innkeeper had suggested, and soon came to the river. Just then he saw a boat pushing off from shore.

He motioned to the men to wait for him, but they seemed to be in a hurry to get on their way. He called after them, but they ignored them and were soon out of sight.

He scanned the river to see if there was another boat. When one appeared Mr. Burchell took off his coat and waved it in the air. Relief swept through him as he watched the boat come toward him.

The men in the boat, however, did not seem eager to have a passenger. They seemed to be debating whether or not to take him aboard. After about ten minutes, they brought the boat to shore. As they came nearer Mr. Burchell noticed that they were rough looking men.

One told him that he could climb in,

ignoring the other's objections. It was not long before Mr. Burchell realized that these men were foul-mouthed and unmannerly. Several whispered to each other. Now and again Mr. Burchell caught a word, and what he heard made him uneasy. Presently Mr. Burchell observed that the boat was headed in the opposite direction from Bristol. He mentioned this to one of the men, who sneered, "Do you think we'll let you go so easily, now that we've caught you? You'll be at the bottom of the river before too much longer!"

At this they all shouted with laughter, adding their own threats and curses.

By now Mr. Burchell was thoroughly alarmed. Obviously, they mistook him for someone else. He had also seen the men occasionally reach for a bottle of liquor from under a tarp, and supposed they were up to no good purpose.

"You are making a big mistake," ventured Mr. Burchell. "Who do you think me to be?"

The men did not answer his question but jeered, "Don't try that game, mister! You know very well what's going on!"

Mr. Burchell tried to assure them that he was not the person they thought he was, but that only made them angry. All he could do now was to ask God for his divine assistance. He then spoke seriously to the men. "If you hurt me in any way, God will judge you for it. He sees everything. He knows I am innocent!"

He saw that the men exchanged questioning glances, but they said nothing.

Mr. Burchell then addressed each man individually, telling them that one day they would have to appear before a holy God and give a full account of their deeds.

At length the man who was evidently the captain cried out, "I can't take this anymore! We've got to let him out! I don't think he's the man we thought he was." Then, turning to Mr. Burchell, he asked, "Where did you want to go, sir?"

"I'd like to be in Bristol as soon as possible," replied Mr. Burchell.

The captain responded, "We can't go as far as that, but we'll go as far as we dare, and then help you to find a way to Bristol."

Mr. Burchell thanked them for their kindness, not forgetting to silently thank the Lord for His intervention. Noting that the men were rather subdued, he took the opportunity of speaking to them about their shameful way of life. He spoke earnestly, and with great concern for their souls. They all appeared to be impressed with his words and concern.

When it was time for Mr. Burchell to step ashore, they refused to take any money, but offered that one of them would accompany him to a farmhouse they knew of.

The two set out together, Mr. Burchell telling him along the way of his need to repent and believe the gospel. The man was so interested in what Mr. Burchell had to say, that he rented a carriage and drove him to Bristol. As a result, Mr. Burchell arrived at the fabric shop just as it opened for business that day. He heartily thanked his companion for his kindness. Mr. Burchell was able to retrieve most of his cloth, and returned home that evening, thankful for God's goodness.

Some years later, Mr. Burchell became a minister, and as he passed through a town, he was approached by a man who introduced himself as the man who had accompanied him to Bristol. Mr. Burchell was amazed at the changed appearance of the man and told him so.

"Oh, sir," said the man, "after your talk to us in the boat, and then to me on the way to Bristol, none of us felt that we could continue as we had been. I have learned to be a carpenter, and am doing very well in this village. I go to church about three or four miles from here. Our captain never forgot to pray for you to his dying day. He was truly changed. He took his widowed mother into his home, and became a good husband and a good father, as well as a good neighbor. Before, everyone was afraid of him. He was such a mean fellow. But afterwards, he was just the opposite. He opened a little store in town so that he could support his family. And what was better, he had prayer meeting and Bible-study meetings in his house and always wanted to be with God's people. As for the others, they found jobs as part of the crew on a freight liner, and were always well-behaved and dependable."

Mr. Burchell was glad to hear this. He was reminded of Isaiah 55:11, "So shall my word be that goeth forth out of my mouth: it shall not return to me void, but it shall accomplish that which I please, and it shall prosper in the thing whereunto I sent it."

Question: What does God deliver us from? Read Psalm 91; 79:8-9; 80:3. Can you find a verse from Psalm 91 in Matthew 4? What is Jesus suffering in this chapter? In Matthew 6:13 what are we told to ask God for? Scripture reading: Daniel 3:1-20.

21. How God Used a Snowdrift

Bertha Schmidt, a godly widow, lived with Karl, her only son, in a pleasant and neat cottage on the shore of the Baltic Sea. Some fearful news reached the people of this quiet village, however. A hostile army was rapidly approaching a nearby city, and would be passing through their area. These soldiers would probably arrive tomorrow, plundering, stealing and destroying whatever was in their path.

Poor Karl busied himself by barricading all the doors and windows and trying to make their little cottage as strong and hard to break into as possible. He worked at a feverish pace. Finally he sank into a chair. His fear, however, was not decreased by all his effort; instead, his fear grew. To make matters worse, a terrible snowstorm was raging, and the wind howled around the little cottage, making strange and eerie noises.

Karl sat in gloomy silence, pale and trembling. His mother, however, was quietly busy. She was calmly reading her Bible and praying to her God. At last she raised her eyes and smiled at her son. She repeated two lines of a well-known poem:

Round us a wall our God shall rear,
And our proud foes shall quail with fear.

Karl stared in disbelief. "Mother, how can you believe that?" he cried. "How can God build a wall around our cottage strong enough to keep out an army?"

"Have you never read that *not a sparrow falls to the ground without His will, Karl?"* she answered quietly. Karl did not answer, but fidgeted uneasily.

During the night, the storm ended. Soon after, Karl heard the fearful sound of the approaching army. Screaming, crashing, and yelling could be heard from their neighbors' cottages. The sound of the uproar came closer and closer. Karl felt sick with fear.

At last, however, the awful sounds died away. The army had passed. Karl didn't dare to move yet. After some hours, he removed the boards from the windows and tried to open the door. It was stuck. After much pushing, he had gotten it open far enough to crawl out. He had to dig his way out and up, for a snowdrift had covered the entire front of the house!

After a lot of effort he climbed over the drift and down onto the road. He stopped there in amazement. He could not believe what he saw! From the road, no house could be seen at all, only a large snowdrift! 'Round us a wall our God shall rear...' he thought. He climbed over the drift.

"Mother!" he called. "Mother! You've got to come outside!"

Karl helped his mother through the door and over the drift. The two of them stood together in the street looking at "God's wall." They wept together for some time, and finally Mrs. Schmidt looked up to heaven and said quietly, "Faithful is He who hath promised. He also hath done it."

God can provide remarkable and immediate answers to prayer in times of need. Are all God's answers to prayer this sudden and remarkable?

Question: Should God's people worry when they are in danger? What should they do instead?
Scripture reading: 2 Kings 7:13-23
*Matthew 10:29.

22. Captain Ryder's Rescue

Captain Ryder owned a large ship which he sailed to make his living. He would carry loads of merchandise from South America to Australia. From there he would take on a new load and sail for China. He had a crew of thirteen men to sail the ship, including a carpenter.

One spring, however, Captain Ryder experienced a serious problem. Seven of his men deserted him upon reaching South America. Now he had to find a new carpenter, as well as six new deck hands. As he began to ask around for help, an official-looking person approached him.

"Say, Captain," the gentleman asked, "I am looking for a ship to take me to Tahiti. Would you have room for me when you set sail?"

"Certainly, sir!" Captain Ryder replied. "We would be honored to have you sail with us! If I am successful with finding new crew members, I hope to sail next Wednesday. Could you be ready by then?"

The gentleman was Governor Wilson. He had been looking for a way to take a large sum of money to the governor of Tahiti. Now he had been promised a place on *The Seven*

Seas, Captain Ryder's ship. Returning to his room, he placed the money in a small chest and hid it in one of his own trunks. "I won't even tell the captain about the money," he thought. "That way, no one will know my secret, and I should have a safe journey."

But Tillie, a girl employed in Governor Wilson's office, knew about the money. Tillie had a bad habit of spending her evenings in evil company. One evening she mentioned to her friends that Governor Wilson had an important secret job to do. She told how much money he was carrying, and that he was going to sail on *The Seven Seas* next Wednesday. Tillie did not know that Harry Jensen was listening to her story! Harry worked as a ship's carpenter, but had been without a job for many months. He looked very respectable, but was involved in all kinds of crime. Hearing Tillie's story, he went to find the captain of *The Seven Seas*. A plan was forming in his evil mind. He was going to be rich at last!

Captain Ryder liked Harry immediately. He was especially pleased to hear that Harry could not only be his carpenter, but that he would bring six men with him to work as deck hands. Everything was quickly arranged, and on Wednesday, *The Seven Seas* set sail as planned. But Captain Ryder quickly discovered that the six new crew members were very rough men. They did not obey orders and did their work very carelessly. Harry was the only one who seemed to work willingly and remain respectful.

After sailing for several days, a bad storm began to batter the ship. To make matters worse, the ship began to leak. "Harry," instructed Captain Ryder, "you must search the ship to find the leak and repair it as quickly a possible!"

After being gone for some time, Harry returned saying, "I'm sorry, Captain! I've searched everywhere, but I cannot find the leak."

"Then man the pumps!" the captain ordered. "We're taking on too much water!" Captain Ryder, who was a godly man, prayed silently to the Lord for His help and guidance.

The crew kept the pumps going day and night, but the leak only seemed to get worse. On the third day, Captain Ryder noticed something tossing on the waves not far from the ship. Looking through his binoculars, he saw that it was a native from one of the nearby islands. He was struggling through the waves in a canoe, desperately trying to reach the ship. Even though he knew it would be dangerous to go back, the captain gave his orders. "Turn the ship! We must go back to rescue that man before he drowns!"

But the new crew members cursed and refused to obey. "We're not going to take chances just to rescue him. He's only an ignorant native, anyway. Let him drown, for all we care!"

Captain Ryder watched as the leaking ship drifted farther away from the canoe. With a prayer in his heart, he went quietly to the back of the ship and dropped an anchor over the side. The dragging anchor slowed the drifting ship. Soon the canoe was near enough for the captain to throw a rope to the struggling native. The man gratefully caught the rope and climbed on board. He was young and very strong so after resting for a short time, he gladly helped with trying to pump water from the ship. But he did not speak to the other men. When asked for his name, he only said "Matt." It seemed that he could not understand or speak English.

The storm continued, and the ship took on more and more water. The captain sadly realized that they would have to leave the sinking ship. As soon as the storm let up, everyone would have to use the long-boats to survive. Captain Ryder began to give orders to stock the long-boats with food. Soon Governor Wilson asked to speak to him. Sitting down in the empty dining room, Governor Wilson spoke quietly, "Captain, I have a very valuable box on board with me. Somehow, I must get it safely to Tahiti!"

As they spoke, the captain noticed that Matt had crept into the room on his hands and knees. Just as he was going to scold him, Matt whispered, "Shh! Wait! Must talk!" Underneath the table where he could not be seen he urgently spoke in broken

English, "Much danger! Men will cut throats! Then money box lost—ship too!"

Governor Wilson was shocked. But he understood what Matt was trying to tell him. Quickly he went to his cabin and loaded his revolver. Matt told the rest of his story to Captain Ryder. "Matt see many things, hear much." He explained how he had seen a row of holes in the side of the ship when he was still in his canoe. He also saw the pumps working and guessed that something was very wrong. He came on board the ship, but pretended that he could not speak English. As he worked with the carpenter and his friends, he heard them discuss their plans. As soon as the longboats were out, Harry and his men planned to kill the captain and the governor. Then they would return to the ship, repair the holes, and make off with the money. They would also sell the ship at the next port, and everyone would be rich.

Captain Ryder quickly armed himself and called his faithful men. The carpenter and his men did not know that their plot had been discovered. Harry and Jake were both asleep in Jake's cabin at the time. Captain Ryder and his men entered their cabin quietly and quickly overpowered them. The other five were easily taken, and soon all seven were securely bound and locked up in the hold of the ship.

Matt quickly led Captain Ryder and his men to Harry's cabin. There were the holes that Harry himself had made! The holes were soon repaired and the ship was pumped dry at last. Four days later, *The Seven Seas* safely reached Tahiti. The criminals were turned over to the proper authorities. Then Captain Ryder and Governor Wilson bought a new whaleboat for Matt as a reward for his service to them. They watched as he set sail back to his own island.

Much time had passed since Captain Ryder and his crew had set sail. *The Seven Seas* was several weeks late for arriving back home. One ship reported having seen them from a distance—about to sink. After several weeks passed, Captain Ryder and his crew were thought to be drowned. This sad news also reached Betty Ryder the good captain's wife, and their two children. During all the anxious days of waiting, she never gave up hope. Each day she earnestly prayed for her husband's safety. At last, however, she began to fear that her dear husband had drowned. Then she knelt down with her children and prayed, "Oh Lord! Thy will be done. Whether he is alive or dead, he is safe in Thy hands."

Poor Betty was worn out from the weeks of anxiety. She wanted to read to her children from the Bible, but she was too overcome. She pointed to the passage she had chosen and asked her daughter, Lucy, to read. Captain Ryder himself was walking up to their door as Lucy's clear voice came through an open window, "Blessed are the

merciful, for they shall obtain mercy."
(Matthew 5:7) Tears filled his eyes. He saw
God's wonderful providence in giving him
the desire to save the life of the young native,
who in turn was used by God to save his
own life and his ship! In a moment, he
entered the happy circle of his dear family.
With unspeakable joy, he told his happy
family the story of how wonderfully God
had cared for him in His marvelous
providence.

Question: Can you name two more
Beatitudes from Matthew 5? How did
Captain Ryder show mercy and how did
he obtain mercy?
Scripture reading: Genesis 19:1-29.

23. "Cling Close to the Rock!"

Once a train was chugging through the Allegheny Mountains. It had reached a place where there was a deep cliff on one side, and a steep wall of rock that went straight up on the other. The train ran very close to this rocky wall. All at once the whistle blasted and the engineer shouted, "Put on the brakes! Stop the train!"

The passengers were alarmed. They looked out of the windows, expecting to see or hear of a disaster. Thankfully, there was not much to see. The engineer had discovered a little girl and her baby brother playing on the tracks in front of the oncoming train. It was impossible to stop the train in time, and it seemed as if the children would be crushed to death. But just at that moment, the girl's eye caught sight of two niches in the wall of the rock, made when blasting a place to lay the tracks. Snatching up her little brother, she pressed her brother into one of the niches, and put herself in the other. While the train went thundering by, the passengers heard the urgent voice of the little girl pleading: "Cling close to the rock, Johnny! Cling close to the rock, and you'll be safe!"

This beautiful story is a wonderful picture of Jesus and His people! Jesus is *the* Rock, and His people are safe in Him. We are exposed to dangers far worse than the little girl and her brother. But if we find a hiding place in the Rock Jesus, we will be safe forever. Those who pray: *Rock of Ages, cleft for me; Let me hide myself in Thee!* will never be disappointed.

Let the water and the blood,
From Thy riven side which flowed,
Be of sin the double cure,
Cleanse me from its guilt and power.

Not the labor of my hands,
Can fulfill Thy law's demands.
Could my zeal no respite know,
Could my tears forever flow,
All for sin could not atone;
Thou must save, and Thou alone.

Nothing in my hand I bring;
Simply to Thy cross I cling;
Naked, come to Thee for dress;
Helpless, look to Thee for grace;
Foul, I to the fountain fly;
Wash me, Savior, or I die.

Augustus Toplady

Question: What incident in the life of Christ is referred to in the first verse of the hymn (John 19:34)? How can you find refuge in *the* Rock, Christ Jesus.
Scripture reading: Isaiah 32:1-8.

24. God is Faithful

It was the day before Christmas, and snow was falling. The biting wind piled the snow in drifts, making travel difficult. Mr. Reiner peered out the window and grumbled, "Why today, of all days? And in this weather! What can be so important that I have to risk my life on a trip to town in this weather? Why couldn't it wait until after the holidays?"

Mrs. Reiner frowned as she listened to her husband. It wasn't like him to complain but she could understand his frustration.

"Whatever the reason, Jacob," she said, "God has your good in mind."

Mr. Reiner did not seem to hear her. He was bundling himself in his warmest clothes, eager to be off as soon as possible in order to make it home before dark.

"Don't worry, Marguerite. If the weather turns worse, I'll stay in town overnight."

Snow swirled into the cabin as Mr. Reiner stepped out into the storm. Still muttering to himself, he closed the door firmly behind him and headed to the barn. Quickly, he hitched the horse to the sleigh. Then he made himself comfortable under the pile of furs, flicked the reins, and off they went.

Mr. Reiner's mood did not improve during the three-hour trip to town. Usually, he was cheerful and pleasant, even when things went wrong. He was a man who feared the Lord. His bad mood today certainly was not becoming for one who served a Master who makes no mistakes.

Although the snow fell steadily, the horse was strong and could pull the sleigh easily through the deep snow. When he reached the office of the forestry services, Mr. Reiner tied his horse to the hitching post, fed and watered it, and covered it with a blanket. When he entered the building, he was surprised to see only the janitor. He had thought there was to be an important meeting. He was even more surprised when he was called into the office of the new supervisor. Mr. Reiner had met him only once, but in that one meeting, he had discovered that this man cared for no one but himself.

"Are you Ranger Reiner?" asked the supervisor bluntly.

"Yes, sir, I am," he answered politely.

"You have worked here for quite some time, I understand," the man continued.

"Yes, sir, by the goodness of God I have worked as a ranger for forty-three years."

"By the goodness of your superiors!" retorted the supervisor angrily. "But the last report you wrote was very poor quality! Your handwriting is barely legible and the report itself is lacking all kinds of information!"

The ranger was shocked. "Sir, no one has ever accused me of anything like this in all the forty-three years I have worked here! I have always done good work and worked hard and have done my best."

Jumping to his feet, the supervisor shouted, "How dare you imply that I am wrong? Your report shows that you know nothing of forestry. You may have worked here for forty-three years, but I don't know what good you ever did! As of today your job here is finished. Merry Christmas," he added with a cruel grin.

Slowly, Mr. Reiner left the office. What an unexpected blow! How painful to be treated so rudely by such a conceited, self-serving man! In a daze, Mr. Reiner untied his horse and made his way back through the deserted streets. He was passing the home of the president of the forestry service, and thought briefly of telling him about the way he had just been treated. "What good will that do?" he mumbled sadly.

Just then the front door of the president's home flew open, and a servant girl ran out. "Sir, this package is for you. There are important papers in here, my master says."

Mr. Reiner thanked the girl and drove on. He put the package in his coat pocket. What did he care anymore? It wasn't his job now, he thought bitterly.

The snow was still falling and the roads were worse than before. Mr. Reiner was too preoccupied with his angry thoughts to be thankful for his strong horse and warm furs. Up ahead, he saw someone plodding through the high drifts. "What fool would be out walking in the snow on a day like this?" he thought indignantly.

When he came closer, he saw it was a woman who carried a young child. They were cold and tired. The woman looked longingly at the sleigh.

"No respectable woman would be out alone on such a day," muttered Mr. Reiner under his breath.

"How far is it to town?" asked the woman breathlessly.

"About six hours walking," answered Mr. Reiner. Heartlessly, he drove on, leaving the woman standing in the deep snow.

Instead of laying his troubles before the Lord, and feeling pity for the woman and her child, Mr. Reiner felt sorry for himself and angry at everyone else. When he arrived home his wife and granddaughter, Greta served him a bowl of steaming rabbit stew. But Mr. Reiner scowled and ate his meal in silence, so they left him alone.

The quiet of the cabin was broken by a soft thud at the door. Greta cautiously opened it and found a little bird on the threshold. "Poor thing," she murmured. "I'll take care of you. You came to the right place. No one is ever treated badly here."

The words hit Mr. Reiner like a physical blow. Suddenly he thought of the woman and her child struggling through the deep snow. Had he really been so cruel? Perhaps they were already dead! Frantically, he pulled on his heavy winter coat and boots.

"Where are you going?" asked his wife and granddaughter.

"I'll be back in two hours at the most."

Before they could answer, he was out the door, running to the barn. A half hour later he passed the place where he had met the woman. She had been going toward town, so she might be a bit farther ahead. All the way, Mr. Reiner had been praying. He had forgotten about his lost job and thought only of his ungodly behavior. How ashamed he was! "Oh Lord, forgive my terrible sins of this day!" he begged. "Please let me find the woman and child alive."

Fifteen minutes later he saw them. It was dark now, and had he not been searching for them, he might have missed them completely. The woman had fallen into the snow. Her child was wrapped in her thin coat. Mr. Reiner scooped them up in his strong arms and lifted them into the sleigh. He wrapped them in the extra blankets and furs he had hurriedly grabbed before heading out. He prayed they would still be alive when they reached home.

Mr. Reiner carried the woman and child into the warm cabin and laid them on the bed. They looked so pale and still. Quickly, Mrs. Reiner and Greta ran to fetch warm, dry clothing. Together, they massaged their patients' icy limbs and periodically dribbled some warm broth into their mouths. Then Greta was sent to bed, and the elderly couple remained by the bedside to care and pray for the mother and her child.

Sometime during the long quiet night, Mrs. Reiner whispered, "They're sleeping peacefully now. And there's no fever. You go to bed, Jacob. I'll sleep here in my chair."

It was late the next morning before the visitors awoke. After eating a little breakfast, the little boy wanted to play, but the woman shyly asked if she could go back to bed.

Finally, after a delicious supper the woman felt well enough to speak with her rescuers. "I wish to thank all of you for your great kindness to me and my son," she said. "I'm so grateful that the Lord put it into your heart to come and get me! If you hadn't, I don't think we'd have made it to town. God is good. He is always faithful."

Another wave of shame rolled over Mr. Reiner. Had he really judged this godly woman as a sinful person unworthy of his help? What a horrible crime is pride!

"I must ask your forgiveness for not stopping when I first passed you. Yes, my dear wife," continued Mr. Reiner with tears, when he saw his wife's shocked look, "I passed by this poor woman. What a mercy that God does not treat us as we treat one another!" His tears flowed, for he wondered again at God's forgiving grace.

A memorable Christmas evening was spent in the little cabin that night. It was bedtime before Mrs. Reiner remembered to ask her husband about his trip to town. Sadly, Mr. Reiner explained what had happened and then he remembered the package. He looked in his coat pocket, but it was gone. "Did you find a brown package, Marguerite?" he asked his wife. "It was in my coat pocket, but now it's missing."

The young woman looked up, startled, "Oh, I forgot! I found a package on the road. I wondered if it could be yours. I was going to bring it to town to find out whose it was. Did you find it in my clothes, Mrs. Reiner?"

"I found something, but I didn't look at it," answered Mrs. Reiner. "I'll go and get it."

She quickly returned with the package and handed it to her husband. He pulled out a letter and read aloud.

Dear Mr. Reiner,

The new supervisor has made several complaints to me about your work, and has requested that a more qualified person take over your job. I have given the matter serious consideration and have decided to find a replacement for you. Therefore, you no longer have the position of ranger.

However, I have personally requested and received permission from the Prince of Germany (as you see in the enclosed official document) to promote you to the position of top ranger in the Black Forest region. Accept my sincere congratulations on your promotion. I wish you and your loved ones

a blessed Christmas and a happy New Year.
Sincerely, Karel Groetenhuis
President of Forestry Services

Tears of shame and gratitude streamed down Mr. Reiner's cheeks. How good God was to such a grumbling, undeserving sinner! While he had been complaining bitterly, God had already provided for him. How great is God's faithfulness! How tenderly the Lord had cared for him! How foolish and selfish he had been! Before they went to bed that night, Mr. Reiner read the familiar passage from the gospel of Luke about the miracle of Jesus' birth. To Mr. Reiner it seemed to be an even greater wonder than ever before. Jesus Christ, the ever-faithful Lord, came to save such selfish, whining, faithless sinners!

"It is of the LORD's mercies that we are not consumed, because his compassions fail not. They are new every morning: great is thy faithfulness" (Lamentations 3:22-23).

Question: In Matthew 19:19, how are we told to treat other people? What warning did the Israelites receive in Obadiah 15? What does Jesus say in Matthew 7:12? If Mr Reiner had remembered these texts when he passed the woman on the road, what would have happened?
Scripture reading: Psalm 89:1-10.

25. Herman's Escape

Herman Franks had been a sailor for several years. He loved the rough life on the seas, and his duties carried him to many parts of the world. But Herman lived very carelessly. He never thought about the possible dangers of his job. He had been brought up by a godly mother. But he pushed all thoughts of the Bible and of eternity from his mind.

One summer Herman's ship was stationed in Africa. They had sailed up a very wide river. But for several days the ship lay at anchor. The intense heat of the tropics made the sailors lazy. Many of them started drinking. Herman, too, was no longer thinking clearly. "Hey, Joe!" he called to another sailor. "I'm going in to cool off. I can easily swim to shore and back. It's not that far. Are you coming, too?"

"I don't think so, Herman. Do you think it's safe?"

But Herman didn't stop to think about the dangers of the river or of the jungle beyond. "It's too hot here for me. I'm going for a dip!"

So saying, Herman dove into the river and began to swim towards shore. The other sailors watching from on deck were almost tempted to follow him. But suddenly, as if from nowhere, a large crocodile rose to the surface of the water and began swimming after Herman. The men spotted it at once and immediately they began to shout a warning. "Herman! Look out! A crocodile is after you!"

Herman turned for just a moment. Seeing the terrible danger he was in sobered him instantly. As the race for life began, the sailors fired shots to try to scare the crocodile away. But nothing helped. The crocodile continued gliding after its prey.

Herman threw all his strength into trying to reach the shore in time. Pictures of a most terrible death floated before his eyes. He swam faster than he had ever swum before. His lungs felt like they were about to burst. But the crocodile was gaining on him.

At last Herman was nearing the shore with the crocodile close behind. Maybe there was hope of reaching the safety of land after all. But just as he thought he was nearly safe, he heard something in front of him. He looked ahead across the last few feet of river. There crouching on the bank in front of him was a snarling tiger waiting to spring! And just behind him was the crocodile. Terrified, Herman looked back. He saw the crocodile open its great jaws to close in for the kill. Ahead, he saw the tiger spring toward him from the shore!

In an instant, Herman realized his greater danger—certain death faced him! In a moment he would have to appear before God. His whole life of sin seemed to pass before his eyes in an instant. He saw that his soul was lost. He had a life of sin behind him and the judgment of God before him. In his trapped position, Herman screamed in terror, "Oh God! Have mercy on me, a terrible sinner!"

Herman's prayer was answered immediately. Dodging frantically to one side, he avoided the flying tiger. But the tiger could not stop and landed right on the crocodile. A terrible death struggle followed. Snarls and screams from the tiger were mixed with thrashing and splashing of the great crocodile. But the teeth and claws of the tiger were no match for the crocodile's iron jaws. The water foamed red with the tiger's blood. Herman watched from shore as the crocodile slowly drew the snarling, struggling tiger under the water. Both disappeared into the deep river. Deeply moved, Herman witnessed what surely would have been his own end.

The sailors watched everything happen from the ship. They were amazed to see their friend so narrowly escape from the jaws and claws of death. They immediately came in a rowboat and brought him back to the ship.

As soon as Herman reached the deck, he fell upon his knees. In a trembling voice, he thanked God for delivering him in such a miraculous way. The sailors stood with bowed heads. Everyone was deeply impressed with what they had just witnessed.

Herman immediately returned to his room and opened his trunk. When he had joined the Navy, his mother had given him a Bible to take with him. This Bible had lain at the bottom of his trunk for years. He had never bothered to open it. But now he took it out and began to read it whenever he could. Herman carried his Bible with him wherever he went. At times other sailors would listen as he read the Word of God.

It pleased the Lord to use this experience for Herman's conversion. Herman was convicted of his lost condition before God. He confessed to God how he had lived in sin for so many years. He was also given to see by grace that the divine Substitute had died in his place. He had been saved from a terrible death in the water. But by grace it became an even greater wonder that he was also saved from eternal death through the work of the Lord Jesus Christ.

Question: Herman was saved three times in one day. In what ways was he saved?
Scripture reading: Psalm 119:65-72.

26. Hidden in the Mist

Many years ago, Christians in Scotland, named Covenanters, were terribly persecuted because of their religion. They were forbidden to meet for worship, and bands of heavily armed soldiers marched throughout the country for the purpose of hunting those who held meetings, in order to imprison them.

One Sunday, a little group of these Covenanters met to worship God in a little valley. During the service, they heard hoofbeats and the clanking of armor, the sound of soldiers coming their way. What could they do? There was no place to hide. So they remained where they were, praying to God to take care of them.

And God did keep them safe. There were mists and clouds scattered over the side of the mountain. These seemed to be floating about, without any guidance. But just before the horsemen came near enough to notice the Covenanters, these clouds gathered, and settled down over the valley in which the Covenanters were assembled. The mists were spread out like a curtain all around them, so that, though the soldiers rode within five hundred feet of the Covenanters, they never saw one of them.

So you see how the Lord protected His dear people. "Whoso hearkeneth unto me shall dwell safely, and shall be quiet from fear of evil" (Proverbs. 1:33)

Question: What was the name of the group of people who were persecuted and what country did they come from? What does God promise to do for those who listen to Him?
Scripture reading: Psalm 124.

27. "It's All for the Best"

When Mary, daughter of Henry VIII, was Queen of England, many people were persecuted and killed because they refused to join the Roman Catholic Church. Some were put in prison, others were chained to the stake and burned to death.

During that time, there lived a faithful minister whose name was Bernard Gilpin. He was fully convinced of the truth the Bible teaches in Isaiah 3:10a: "Say ye to the righteous, that it shall be well with him," and in Romans 8:28: "And we know that all things work together for good to them that love God, to them who are the called according to his purpose." Reverend Gilpin believed this so completely, that whenever something happened to him, he would say, "It's all for the best."

One day, during Queen Mary's reign, he received a summons to go to London to be tried by those who were putting the Protestants to death. When he left home, his friends thought they would never see him again in this world. But on his way to London, he fell and broke his leg. In those days, breaking a leg was quite serious. They didn't have the medical supplies and knowledge we have today. Reverend Gilpin had to stay where he was. He could not travel for several months while he waited for his leg to heal.

Somebody said to him, "Do you think this is all for the best?"

"I have no doubt of it," he answered.

While Reverend Gilpin was waiting for his leg to heal, Queen Mary died. Her sister Elizabeth became queen of England in her place. She was a Protestant, and the persecution which had been carried on during the reign of her sister was stopped at once. Reverend Gilpin returned home as soon as he could travel again, instead of going to London to be put to death. His broken leg was the means of saving his life. His faith was not put to shame, for God's promises are true and eternal.

Perhaps there are things that have happened in your life that you do not understand. If you are not God's child, these difficulties are God's callings to you to repent and turn to Him for salvation. If you obey His voice, then these things will be for your good. Not listening to God, and refusing to obey Him, however, will result in your everlasting destruction. How loving and kind the Lord is in warning us and giving us time to repent!

If you are God's child, and there are things which have happened to you that you do not understand, trust that the Lord does all things perfectly, and for your good. Remember that we do not deserve any good at all, and the good things He gives us are mercies. When the Lord sends difficulties and trials, remember that He gives them out of His fatherly hand. We may not understand why we have so many difficulties, but trust the Lord to work them all out for His glory and for our good. "Now no chastening for the present seemeth to be joyous, but grievous: nevertheless afterward it yieldeth the peaceable fruit of righteousness unto them which are exercised thereby" (Hebrews. 12:11).

Question: Who shall it be well with in Isaiah 3:10? How did Reverend Gilpin's broken leg work for his good?
Scripture reading: Romans 8:28-39.

28. John Reynolds

John Reynolds and his mother were very poor. John's father had died several months ago, and they had no money. One day, John said to his mother, "I've tried to find a job, but there is no work to be found. I've decided to go to sea, and earn some money that way."

Mrs. Reynolds was not happy with this idea, but she understood that there was no other choice. So she kissed him goodbye after a parting prayer.

Off he went with his little bundle, and his Bible in his pocket. He walked to the nearest seaport town, to try to get a job on board a ship. He went from vessel to vessel among the docks for several days, but could not find a job. At last, when he was ready to give up, he saw the captain of a ship passing by.

"Sir, do you need a boy to work for you?" asked John eagerly.

"That's exactly what I need," answered the captain with a smile.

"Please hire me, sir! I need a job," pleaded John.

"Alright, show me your references," said the captain.

John's shoulders sagged. "I don't have references, sir. Nobody knows me in this town. In my own town, I could get references in a minute, though."

"Sorry, I don't hire people without references." The captain turned to leave.

Suddenly, John had an idea. "Wait!" he called. "What about this?"

Turning back, the captain saw John holding out his Bible. On the front page it read, "Presented to John Reynolds, for good behavior in Sunday School."

"How long did it take you to earn this Bible?" asked the captain.

"A whole month, sir," said John.

"Good, you're hired. Come with me."

John followed the captain to his ship. Soon they were on their way to St. Petersburg. During the voyage, a dreadful storm arose. The wind blew fiercely and everyone expected the ship to go down. The sailors had done all they could and were simply waiting for the end. Huddled below the deck, with a lantern in one hand and his Bible in the other, John began to read Psalm 51 aloud. One by one the sailors gathered around him. When he finished, John prayed aloud, asking God to have mercy on them and to spare them.

God heard John's prayer. The storm was soon over and they made their way safely into port. The captain was so grateful that he promised everyone a day off when they reached their destination.

John was glad to have a day off. He was so busy on the ship, running errands for the captain and whoever needed him, that he was happy to spend a day as he pleased. He decided to visit the beautiful city of St. Petersburg. He watched as rich people rode up to the palace and were welcomed by the royal servants. As he stood watching in wonder, observing carriage after carriage pass by, something dropped at his feet. It was a bracelet, sparkling with jewels. Obviously, it had dropped from a wealthy woman's carriage. John picked it up, and called after the coachman to stop, but the noise and bustle of the people around him, drowned out John's voice.

Uncertain what to do, John returned to the ship with the bracelet, and showed it to the captain.

"You're a very lucky boy," said the captain, examining the sparkling bracelet. "Those are diamonds, you know."

"But it's not mine," stated John firmly.

"How did you get it?" asked the captain.

"It fell in front of me when a carriage passed by. I picked it up and called after the driver, but he didn't hear me."

"Then you did all you could, and it now belongs to you," said the captain.

"No, sir," John shook his head, "it is not mine."

"You're a foolish boy. Give the bracelet to me, and I'll sell it for you when we get home. You'll be a very rich boy."

"Yes, but it isn't mine," repeated John. "What if we were to run into another storm on the way home, what then?"

The captain was quiet for a moment. "You're right. I hadn't thought about that. Well, then we must try to find the owner of this bracelet." It took a bit of work, but at last the captain and John were able to find the owner. She was so glad to have her bracelet back that she gave John a large sum of money as a reward for being honest. When he returned home to his mother, he bought her a cozy little home, and made sure she was well cared for.

Later, John became a captain himself. He was successful in his business, but he never forgot to be obedient to God who had provided so well for him and his mother.

Question: There is a word in Philippians 4:8 that is also in the story you have just read. What is it?
Scripture reading: Acts 27.

29. Lost!

One cold, wintry afternoon, Willie was sent to deliver a message for his parents. He had to walk about three miles. As he started out the snow began to fall very fast. However, Willie bravely hurried on. At last he was able to deliver his message and soon he was on his way home again.

As he started back, Willie walked as fast as he could, but the snow fell faster and began blowing into drifts. To make matters worse, night was coming and he was still far from home. The snow was soon more than knee-deep, making it very difficult to continue. As darkness fell, Willie could no longer see where he was going, and soon strayed from the path. He was lost!

Willie stumbled on through the horrible darkness, fighting his way against bitterly cold wind and blinding snow. However hard he tried, he could not find his path again. He no longer had any idea where he was going, and his strength was beginning to fail as he struggled on through the storm.

Suddenly Willie fell into a deep hollow which had drifted full of snow. There he lay up to his chest in snow, unable to get out.

The more he struggled, the deeper he sank. To make matters even worse, Willie realized that the snow was becoming deeper all the time. Soon it would cover him entirely! All hope of escape seemed to be cut off, and there was only one thing left to do – cry for help! Willie's half-choked voice began to call out, "Lost! Lost! Lost!" Not knowing whether anyone would be able to hear him, Willie continued calling as loudly as he could with his failing strength.

When Willie did not return home, his parents became very worried. His father decided to go out to search for him. He soon found how impossible it was to find anything in the dark, stormy night. After searching in vain for more than an hour, the father was thoroughly exhausted and began to fear that he would have to give poor Willie up as lost. But listen! He heard a faint sound in the distance: "Lost! Lost! Lost!" Was it only the echo of his own thoughts?

He listened carefully and heard the voice again—more distinctly this time. "Lost! Lost! Lost!" It was Willie's voice. Joyfully the father shouted to Willie to keep calling so he could follow the sound. He soon found the treacherous hollow where poor Willie was helplessly trapped, and with much time and great effort, he rescued his dear son who had so narrowly escaped death. Great thankfulness and joy flooded through Willie when he was rescued and safely returned to his home. Never before had his humble home looked so inviting nor his parents seemed so dear to him.

Willie's experience in this true story can serve as a picture of the spiritual experience of conversion. When God begins to work savingly in people's hearts, they begin to see their sinfulness and to fight against it. But eventually their sin overpowers them and they experience their totally lost condition. All their efforts only sink them deeper in the pit of sin. Then they begin to cry out in prayer, "Lost! Lost! Lost!" What surprise, joy and love is experienced when God the Father "finds" His lost children, and delivers them through Jesus Christ! What thankfulness fills their hearts when they are saved and restored!

Some people experience these things in a short and sudden way, as Paul in the Bible. For others it is more slow and gradual as with Timothy. The length of time does not matter, but *conversion must be real in our lives.*

Question: Can you think of two other people in Scripture who were stuck inside pits? Look up the following Scriptures to find out: Genesis 37:23-28; Jeremiah 38. Why is it important for us to experience that we are "lost" in sin before we "find" salvation in Christ?
Scripture reading: Acts 9:1-9.

30. Only One Mediator

A young soldier in the Civil War was caught asleep at his guard post. His punishment was that he had to be shot to death for his carelessness. This young man had a friend who was a lawyer. The lawyer came to visit the imprisoned soldier and asked him how he could have been so careless as to fall asleep.

"Well," said the young soldier, "I could hardly help it. I had been on duty for twenty-four hours. There was no one to replace me, and I was very tired."

The lawyer took this information to the court-martial and pleaded with high officials to drop the death sentence. Sadly, they told him that no one could change the decision except the Commander-in-Chief of the Army, who was Abraham Lincoln, the President of the United States.

The officials gave the condemned soldier some papers to identify himself, as well as an explanation of the sentence and the reasons for the request of change in the sentence. So the young soldier set out for Washington. But along the way, he was robbed and beaten. The thieves took his papers and his money, so that all he had were the dirty, torn clothes he wore. Desperate, he continued to Washington and tried to persuade the guards that he needed to see the Commander-in-Chief of the Army. No one would listen to the poor soldier. In despair, he sat on a bench near the White House and sobbed, with his head in his hands. Presently, a boy saw the weeping man and asked him, "Sir, what's the matter?"

The man looked up and shook his head sadly. "You're just a child and can't help me. I won't bother you with my troubles."

But the boy did not give up. "Tell me anyway, sir. Maybe I can help you."

So the young soldier told the boy his sad story of how he was caught asleep at his guard post and sentenced to death unless the President would change the sentence, but he had no papers to identify himself. All hope of life was gone.

The boy listened very quietly, and then exclaimed, "I can get you in to see the President! I am Tad Lincoln!" He took the man by the hand and led him into the White House. They came to the big doors behind which the President was seated. When Tad tried to open the doors, however, two guards stopped him.

But the boy protested. "My father told me to enter at any time I choose; he will see me anytime." So they entered.

There behind the desk sat the President. The young man, conscious of his rags, stood behind the boy as he was introduced to Mr. Lincoln. At the boy's urging, he told his story again, with tears. The President listened carefully, and when the young man had finished his story, he set him free, giving him a full and complete pardon. Of course, that young man never forgot it.

Boys and girls, that is just what God the Father does for every sinner who comes to Him by Christ. God cannot be approached except through the Son, just as the young soldier could not have gained entrance into the President's room without the President's son. Jesus pardons that sinner and sets him free in Himself. And that saved sinner never forgets it!

Question: Who is the only way to approach God the Father? Can you prove that from Scripture?

Scripture reading: Hebrews 4:14-16.

31. Rock of Ages

Heather McDonald lived in a small village in the northern part of Scotland. One beautiful spring day, she decided to visit her friend in a nearby village. Heather dressed Robbie, her baby boy, and set out on the two-hour walk to her friend's house. Wild flowers were already blooming and the trees were full of buds. All signs of winter were gone. Heather enjoyed the beauty of God's creation as she walked along.

After spending a pleasant afternoon with her friend, Heather started walking home again. Part way home, she noticed clouds beginning to move in from the north. The air began to get chilly, and she hurried on her way. But as she was crossing the empty fields, large snowflakes began to cover everything. A terrible, unexpected snowstorm was upon her. No houses were in sight and her own home was still about three miles away. Soon the snow reached past her ankles. A cold wind began to blow.

Heather's plaid scarf and jacket were not warm enough to keep out the cold. Realizing their danger, Heather began to run. Hugging little Robbie tightly to keep him as warm as possible, she hurried on through the deepening snow. Heather lifted her heart to the Lord in prayer. "Oh Lord! Help me! Please save us from this awful storm!"

The temperature was still dropping, and the snow made her stumble time and again. Soon the snow became a blinding blizzard as she struggled forward. Just as she felt that she could not go on, Heather came to a narrow valley. She knew that a village was a short way to her left. But her strength was gone and Robbie was beginning to cry from the bitter cold. Desperately, Heather stopped to decide what to do. She could no longer struggle through the deep snow. Robbie was becoming too heavy to carry and he was shaking from the cold. Looking up, Heather noticed a hollow place in a large rock nearby. With a prayer in her heart for her poor child's safety, Heather made her brave decision. Quickly removing her jacket, she wrapped it around her son and carried him to the hollow in the rock. Carefully she laid him inside where he was sheltered from the wind. Then she removed her scarf and tucked it around him. With a sob, Heather turned away from her son. "Oh Lord," she prayed, "please protect my son. I leave him in Thy care!"

The next morning, the storm had passed and many of the men from the area went out to search for those who were missing. Many people lost there lives in that terrible storm. As they searched the fields, they found the body of a young woman without a coat. They immediately recognized Heather, whom they all knew and respected. As they sadly stood with bowed heads, they heard a feeble cry. They looked up in surprise and immediately began to look for what sounded like a baby. They followed the sound to the rocks at the edge of the valley. Then looking up, one man spotted a bit of plaid scarf in an opening of one of the rocks. Rushing to the hollowed rock, the men found little Robbie, carefully wrapped in his mother's jacket, with her scarf tucked in all around him. The men sadly returned to the village with the body of Heather and little Robbie still wrapped in the jacket and scarf.

Heather was deeply mourned by the villagers. Her husband had died a short time before, and Robbie was all she had left. She was well-known in the village and deeply respected by all. She had often testified of her trust in the Lord and had given Him the honor due unto His Name.

Heather's friends could only guess what had happened in that terrible storm. They were deeply moved to think of Heather giving her life in a last attempt to save her son. Many people attended the funeral to see their dear friend laid in her final resting place.

Heather had no relatives, but Hannah, her God-fearing friend, took little Robbie into her own home. She knew that Heather would have wanted her son to be brought up in the fear of the Lord. As Robbie grew, Hannah told him stories from the Bible and taught him to pray. She brought him to church and regularly taught him lessons from God's Word.

Hannah also told him about his own mother as soon as he was old enough to understand. But Robbie heard the story so often that it did not impress him much. In spite of Hannah's loving and careful teaching, Robbie began to keep company with bad friends. Soon he was involved in all kinds of trouble. By the time he had finished school, he was involved in various types of crime. At last, he was arrested and put in jail for seven years. Poor Hannah was heartbroken. It seemed that her prayers and the prayers of Robbie's mother were all in vain.

When Robbie finally got out of jail, he joined the Army. A war was being fought at the time and he was sent to the battlefield. After fighting for many months, one day Robbie received a wound in his leg and had to be taken to the hospital. Infection set in and his leg had to be taken off. Now he had to lie on his back day after day in terrible pain. At last Robbie began to think about home; he remembered the story of how his mother had given her life for him.

One day as Robbie was lying in the hospital, a nurse came to tend another man in his room. After speaking to this man, she began to sing for him. The words of the chorus caught Robbie's attention:

Rock of Ages, cleft for me
Let me hide myself in Thee.

These words struck Robbie's heart. The nurse, seeing that he was upset, came to speak to him. "What is the matter, Robbie?" she asked.

"Oh, nurse!" cried Robbie, "the song you sang just now reminded me of how my mother saved my life when I was a baby. She hid me in the cleft of a rock to save me from a terrible storm. She even wrapped me in her own jacket and scarf, and then froze to death while trying to go for help!"

The nurse saw her opportunity to tell Robbie about the Savior, the Lord Jesus Christ, who gave His own life so that He could be the Rock of Safety for His people. Robbie was deeply impressed, and the nurse hoped that God would apply this message savingly to his heart.

But soon Robbie was strong and well again. He was fitted with a wooden leg and left the hospital. Before long, he returned to his old ways. Living a sinful life, he roamed from town to town. At last he decided to visit the place where he was born. Nothing looked familiar to him, but he decided to look for his mother's grave before he left. The next day, on Sunday, he limped to the churchyard to look for her grave. He was pleased to see that her grave was carefully tended. But as he stood looking down on the grave of the one who had given her life for him, other thoughts began to fill his heart. He remembered verses from the Word of God that he had learned long ago. These verses convicted him of his sin. Robbie felt how worthless he was in the sight of God. With bowed head, he followed the villagers into the church. There he heard a minister preach about the Savior who had given His life to save worthless sinners. Weeping bitterly, Robbie sank down in the pew. "Oh, Lord! Have mercy on me. I am worthless in Thy sight and do not deserve Thy mercy!"

The Lord answered Robbie's prayer. He lived for only five more years, but during that time he was able to testify what the Lord had done for his soul. He was often heard singing:

> Rock of Ages, cleft for me,
> Let me hide myself in Thee.

Question: What started Robbie on the wrong road and turned him away from God's ways? What drew him back?
Scripture reading: John 10:11-18.

32. Saved by a Lamb

This is an old but true story of a man who was traveling in Germany. In one of the villages was a church with an unusual stone carving. Near the top of the tower the man saw a lamb carved from stone. "I wonder why they put that lamb up there?" the man said.

"I'll tell you why," answered a citizen of the town. And this is the story he told.

One day when the church was being built long ago, a workman fell from the scaffold high up around the tower. The men working with him saw him fall and were paralyzed with fear. As quickly as possible, they got down from the scaffold and looked for their fellow worker. They were expecting a horrible sight, for they were sure he had been dashed to pieces. But to their great surprise, their companion was not hurt! A flock of sheep was being guided past the church at the exact moment of the man's fall. He had fallen on one of the lambs. The lamb was crushed to death, but the man was saved.

The carved figure of a lamb was placed on the tower not only to remember and celebrate the providence of God, but also to remind the people of the Son of God who came into this world to die as the Lamb of God in the place of every sinner who comes to Him. "He was wounded for our transgressions, he was bruised for our iniquities" (Isaiah 53:5).

Question: Isaiah wrote these Words of God in Isaiah 53:5 hundreds of years before the death and resurrection of Jesus Christ. What is the special name given to God's Word in instances like this?
Scripture reading: John 1:29-34.

33. The Banker's Story

A Christian man, who lived near a large city, had a sixteen year old son. The father wanted his son to find a job in one of the city banks. After some time, the father found his son a good job in a bank. When he returned home, he told his son about his new job.

"David, I have found you a good job. You will begin on Monday. I want you to be obedient, helpful, and respectful to all those around you. This job is a good opportunity for you. Do your very best in your work. But above all, do not forget the Lord.

"Thank you," answered David. "I'm looking forward to my new job."

David did his best, and was respectful and honest. His employers thought a lot of him. He was promoted several times, until he became the manager of the bank. The key to the safe was in David's possession. It was his duty to see that the money was locked away safely at the end of each day.

One day, a friend of David's told him that he knew how to earn a lot of money by investing ten thousand dollars.

"Thanks, John," answered David, "but I haven't got that much money to invest."

"Sure you do!" responded John. "You work in a bank. You have the key. All you do is borrow this money, and when you've earned this money back, you just return it to the bank. No one will know, plus you will have made a lot of money for yourself."

"No, John," replied David firmly. "That would be wrong. I couldn't do that."

Later that night, when John had left, Satan came and tempted David. It was such a good plan that John had proposed. What could be wrong with borrowing the money? He certainly intended to return it!

At first David resisted the temptation, but after struggling with it for a while, he gave in, and made up his mind to take the money. David knew better. He had been raised by godly parents, and he himself took these things seriously. When David was a young boy, his mother had done her best to teach him about the Lord. She wanted to impress upon him the truth that God is everywhere present. She bought a poster beautifully illustrated with the text, "Thou God seest me." (Genesis 16:13) She hung this in David's bedroom.

At the end of the following day, David was alone in the bank, making preparations to close the bank for the day. He went into the vault, and looked at the money. He picked up a bundle, but no sooner had he picked it up, than he thought of that poster in his room. "Thou God seest me."

Instantly, David threw the bundle back.

Dropping to his knees, he wept, "Oh, Lord, save me from this great sin! Forgive me!"

Getting up from his knees, he finished locking up, and went home.

The first thing David did the following morning was to speak to the president of the bank. He told the man everything.

"I think I should quit my job here," concluded David. "I'm not trustworthy, sir."

The president studied David. "I would like you to stay," he said at last. "God has kept you from giving in to the temptation, and He will keep you safe in the future. If you continue doing your job well, I will not mention this to anyone."

David thanked him with tears in his eyes. He had learned that we need the Lord to help us every day. In our own strength, we cannot fight against sin. We need the Lord Jesus to wash away our sin, and to help us flee from sin. Ask the Holy Spirit to teach you this, too.

Question: Can you think of instances in the Bible where people have committed a sin when they thought that no one had seen, but God had? Joshua 7; Acts 5. When you are tempted to sin, do you ask God to keep you from falling into it? In Jude 24, what do Christians have to look forward to?
Scripture reading: Genesis 16.

34. The Little Slave Girl

Long, long ago (about 1700 years ago), in the fourth century, there were people called the Iberians. They lived in what was once the eastern part of Russia. The Iberians were heathens who had never heard of God.

These people were also ruthless warriors, fighting fierce battles with surrounding tribes and taking young captives to sell as slaves. That is how Nunnia came to live among the Iberians. She was the daughter of a missionary couple who were working with a neighboring tribe. They had been praying for a way to reach the Iberians, but God answered those prayers in a manner far differently from what they had imagined!

The Iberians made war against this tribe and took Nunnia captive. She was then sold as a slave to a respectable Iberian family. It was a terrible day for Nunnia, for she thought she would never see her family again. But God was her heavenly Father, and Jesus her Elder Brother, so she found comfort and strength in her Savior.

Quietly and willingly Nunnia did her work, often doing more than was asked of her. The little slave girl's helpfulness and faithful service were highly appreciated, for not many Iberians were honest or kind. Everyone who came into contact with Nunnia grew to love and respect her, for she was kind, cheerful, polite, and eager to please.

One day Nunnia watched as a father and a mother carried a sick child from house to house.

"Why are they doing that, my lady?" Nunnia asked her mistress.

"It is a custom among our people," explained the lady. "The parents of the sick child are hoping someone will know how to cure their child."

Together they watched as the family approached their home. "Can you help us?" pleaded the father. "We have asked everyone else!"

Sadly, Nunnia's mistress shook her head. "I cannot," she said softly.

With tears in her eyes, the mother of the sick child turned to Nunnia. "Perhaps you know of a cure from your country? Can you help us?"

Nunnia looked at the child. He was very pale and still. "I'm only a girl," she replied. She looked again at the child. Then she lifted her eyes to meet the hopeless gaze of the mother. "But I know someone who can help," she smiled.

"Oh, tell us!" cried the parents eagerly. "Where can we find him? Who is he?"

"He is the great and mighty Lord of

heaven and earth," said Nunnia. "He is almighty and He will help those who seek Him. He is full of compassion and love."

"Can you go get this god?" asked the father, for he thought this God was just another idol.

"Yes," said Nunnia simply. Then she turned and went to her room and knelt by her bed. "Lord," she prayed, "show Thyself for Thine own glory, and help these people!"

Knowing in her heart that God had heard her prayer, she happily returned to the waiting parents. Overjoyed they watched as the little boy opened his eyes and smiled. He was healed! Laughing for joy, they thanked Nunnia and headed for home, telling everyone they met of the miracle that had taken place.

Nunnia was glad that the child was healed, but her joy soon faded when she realized that no honor was given to God who had healed the little boy. Rather, the people honored the slave girl; they believed she was a goddess of some kind with special powers. Soon everyone in the village was talking about the miraculous healing, and before long even the occupants of the royal palace had heard the story.

Not long after this, the Queen of the Iberians became ill, and she thought about the little slave girl. Calling a servant, she commanded, "Fetch the slave girl who healed the child, and bring her to me."

Soon the messengers arrived at the home where Nunnia lived. Bowing low, they respectfully asked her to accompany them to the royal palace to heal the queen. Nunnia was not happy!

"No! No!" she cried. "Do not bow to me! The Lord is God! He is the One you must honor!" Tears rolled down her cheeks, for she was very troubled. "I cannot go with you. I will pray for the queen, but it is God who can heal her, not me."

The queen was very disappointed when the messengers returned without Nunnia, but she was determined to meet the slave girl. After a moment's thought, she called a few servants and ordered them to prepare for a journey to Nunnia's village.

When the queen arrived, beautifully dressed and having so many splendidly dressed servants, Nunnia grew fearful. But the queen was kind, and spoke gently. "Nunnia," she said, "can you heal me, as you healed the little boy?"

"Not I, my lady, but God is the Healer. I will ask Him."

And so, once again, Nunnia prayed to the only One who can help. "Oh Lord in heaven, show the queen that Thou art the almighty God. Heal her of her sickness, and draw her to Thyself."

She returned to the queen, who was smiling. She too was healed! Miraus, the king, was overjoyed when his queen returned in excellent health. "I will send this slave girl a gift," he stated happily.

"Oh, no, don't do that!" protested the queen.

"But why not? She healed you!" answered Miraus incredulously. "She deserves a gift!"

"She's a mysterious child," responded the queen thoughtfully. "Somehow I think she would be offended if you did that. She didn't want my thanks. She only wants us to worship her God."

King Miraus was astonished. "How can anyone refuse riches?" he wondered. But he soon forgot the little slave girl and her strange ways. After all, he didn't know her God, and he was content with his life as it was.

Some weeks later, the king hosted a hunting party on the castle grounds. They divided into groups, and each group went off in a different direction. King Miraus wanted to hunt alone so he took only a servant with him as he entered the forest.

He hadn't gone far when he noticed fresh animal tracks. Instructing his servant to wait for him, he followed the tracks soundlessly. He was so intent on tracking his game, that he became lost in the forest. A heavy fog rolled in, muffling any calls he might have heard from his friends or servants. The more he tried to find his way back, the thicker the fog, and the more eerie the forest became.

Evening was coming on and the king was angry and embarrassed that he was still lost. He sounded his horn, but the only reply was the fog-muffled echoes from the surrounding cliffs. The king became frightened, but suddenly he remembered something his wife had said about the little slave girl.

"The God she serves is a God beyond my understanding," the queen had said. She had added, "Nunnia says He's an invisible God and that He is present everywhere. How can that be, Miraus? And she said He helps those who seek Him. I'd like to know more about this God."

At the time King Miraus had simply shrugged his shoulders and then changed the subject. But now, here in the dense, foggy forest, he thought about this amazing God. "If it is true that this God is everywhere, and that He helps those who seek Him, then I will ask Him to help me."

Then, in the middle of the forest, the king prayed, "Oh Thou whom the slave girl calls her God, if Thou art almighty, show it now and help me! If Thou wilt help me find my way out of this forest, my heart, my life, and all that I have shall be Thine."

The king opened his eyes and stood up. He was amazed to see that the dark mist began to fade and the sky became colored with a beautiful sunset. Awestruck, he quickly found his way through the woods and returned home safely. He was deeply affected and told his wife all that had happened. The queen was also deeply impressed. Both of them now believed that Nunnia's God was the true and living God, for they had both experienced Him to be so.

The very next morning they set out to visit Nunnia, for they thought she would love to hear the wonderful story. The three of them shed tears, and thanked the great God in heaven for His help. Then the king and the queen held Nunnia's hands and asked her to tell them more about this God.

From that moment the royal couple were seen sitting like teachable children beside the lowly slave girl, while Nunnia told them in her simple way all that she knew of her Savior and His wonderful works. The king and queen listened eagerly, and a love for this Savior grew in their hearts.

The king and queen did not forget what they had learned. In fact, they decided that everyone in their kingdom needed to know this God and His Son, Jesus Christ. So the king preached to the men and the queen spoke to the women, and the Lord blessed the messages. The Holy Spirit entered the hearts and homes of many heathen people who now sang the praises of the one true God.

"I will call them my people, which were not my people; and her beloved, which was not beloved. And it shall come to pass, that in the place where it was said unto them,

Ye are not my people, there shall they be called the children of the living God" (Romans. 9:25-26).

Question: Who else protested in the same way as the slave girl when people praised them for doing miracles in God's name? Acts 10:25; Acts 14
Scripture reading: Genesis 41:1-45.

35. The Man and the Tiger

Sir John Gayer was once the mayor of London, England. He loved to travel. Once he made a trip to Asia, and as he passed through a dangerous piece of jungle, he found himself face to face with a fierce-looking tiger. Sir Gayer was all alone, since the rest of his friends had gone on ahead, but he feared the Lord, and although he was frightened, he did not panic. He thought about Daniel, and how God protected him in the lion's den. He believed this same God could help him now. Right there in the middle of the path, Sir Gayer dropped to his knees and asked God to take care of him and save him from the ferocious tiger.

When he had finished his prayer, Sir Gayer opened his eyes and looked around. He was all alone. The tiger was gone.

Do you have a danger on your path? Is there something which frightens you, or seems too hard to overcome? Perhaps you struggle in school; maybe someone teases you constantly; or possibly life at home is not pleasant. The Lord is willing and able to help you: "Call upon me in the day of trouble: I will deliver thee, and thou shalt glorify me"

(Psalm 50:15). The poet William Cowper once wrote: "Satan trembles when he sees the weakest saint upon his knees."

Perhaps you struggle with eternal things and wonder if God is willing to save you. Do you think you have sinned too much? Do you wonder if God listens to children? Are you confused about spiritual things? Do you long to be converted, but it seems God doesn't answer you? The Lord promises salvation to those who seek Him. Do not give up. Continue to seek the Lord, for then you will be blessed. Psalm 34 is full of promises to those who seek the Lord. "The eyes of the LORD are upon the righteous, and his ears are open unto their cry." "The righteous cry, and the LORD heareth, and

delivereth them out of all their troubles."
"The LORD redeemeth the soul of his
servants: and none of them that trust in him
shall be desolate" (Psalm 34:15, 17, 22).

When God inclines the heart to pray,
He hath an ear to hear;
To Him there's music in a groan,
And beauty in a tear.
The humble suppliant cannot fail
To have his wants supplied,
Since He for sinners intercedes,
Who once for sinners died.

Benjamin Beddome

Question: In Psalm 34 who is God
looking at and who is he listening to?
Scripture reading: Judges 14:1-6.

Prayer Points

Honoring God

1.   ★ Ask the Lord to show you how to live a godly life.
⌘ Pray that God will teach you thay sin is never worth its consequences.

2.   ★ Ask God to convict you of pride and selfishness and to make you a cheerful giver. Pray that God will make you generous with your time and the other material blessings He has given you.
⌘ Ask God to show you that He wants you to give Him most of all, your life, heart and love.

3.   ★ Thank God for giving mankind the knowledge of God and His salvation through His Word. Ask Him to give you wisdom and understanding of it.
⌘ Ask God for forgiveness for the times when you have doubted Him and when you do not give Him the respect He deserves.

4.   ★ Ask God to give you a generous, self-sacrificing attitude to others and to God's kingdom.
⌘ Ask God to convict you of the desperate need you have for Christ the Savior.

5.   ★ Thank God for the gift of one day in seven to rest and worship Him. Ask God to help you keep His Word fresh in your mind.
⌘ Ask for forgiveness for negelcting God's day and resenting time that specifically belongs to Him and not you. Ask God to give you a worshipful nature on His day.

6.   ★ Ask God for godly principles in your life as well as the courage to stand up for them in the face of opposition. Ask God to help you love your enemies and those people who are spiteful and nasty to you. Thank God for loving you when you didn't love Him.
⌘ Submit your life entirely to Christ and ask Him to give you the words to say when faced with arguments and temptations from unbelievers. Ask Him to help you believe His Word.

7.   ★ Ask God to make you a good example to non Christians. Ask Him to make your life one that will attract others to Christ. Thank Him for providing for those who obey Him.
⌘ Ask God that you will not be influenced by unbelievers to break His law.

8.   ★ Thank God for those people who He uses to keep you safe: parents, teachers, police, fire service, ambulance people.
⌘ Ask God to deliver you from sin and hell and thank Him for His daily acts of mercy and grace, even though you aren't following Him as you should.

9.   ★ Pray that your family will belong to God and that you will be a godly example to future generations.
⌘ Pray that you will not turn away from the Lord. Pray that God will convict you of the need of your soul without Christ.

10.   ★ Pray that the Lord will keep you constant in your faith despite any troubles and difficulties in your life.
⌘ Pray that God will make your life one that obeys Him no matter what.

11.	★ Pray for those who are in positions of power and authority in your nation. Pray that they will honor God in their lives and policies and that governments will respect God's commands.
⌘ Pray that God will protect you from a life of selfish ambition and that He will show you the immense value of the eternal soul and the fleeting nature of popularity and riches.

12.	★ Pray that God will protect your mouth from speaking evil. Ask Him to give you words of truth and love for Him.
⌘ Ask for forgiveness for the times you spoke against God or did not speak up for Him. Ask forgiveness for when you have used God's name in a flippant or irreverent way and pray for a new heart that will lead to new obedience to God.

13.	★ Ask God to give you strength of soul and character to defeat discouragement. Ask Him to give you a thankful heart at all times.
⌘ Ask the Lord to take away any resentful and bitter thoughts when troubles come. Ask Him to guide you to His own perfect peace.

14.	★ Thank God for the gifts He has given you. Bless His name for the spiritual blessings of salvation and forgiveness.
⌘ Ask God to take away your love of sin and replace it with a love for Him and His word. Ask Him to show you how every good thing comes from Him.

15.	★ Thank God for all your food such as simple fruit and bread and plenty of water to drink. Ask Him to give you a thankful and ungreedy nature towards food.

162

⌘ Pray to God for forgiveness of your sins and ask Him to give you a spiritual hunger to meet with Him and learn about Him every day.

16. ★ Thank God for providing for you in so many wonderful ways—beyond your basic needs. Thank Him for His abundance of love. Ask Him to continue providing for your spiritual needs and to bring you to greater spiritual maturity. ⌘ Pray to the Lord that He will show you His power to save and convict you of your need to be rescued from sin, death and hell.

17. ★ Thank God that He is faithful and unchanging and that whatever happens you can trust in His unfailing love, truth and strength. ⌘ Ask God to show you how meaningless your possessions are and how everything on this earth will pass away but that He and His word will always be there.

18. ★ Ask God to teach you from His Word so that you will teach the truth to future generations and strengthen Christ's church and kingdom. ⌘ Ask God to make you believe in Him with a strong certainty and plead with Him to help you conquer your doubts and unbelief.

19. ★ Thank God that you need not be anxious or worried about what tomorrow may bring because you know that the eternal, just, loving and almighty God will be there, with you, to assist you in all circumstances. ⌘ Ask God to give you conviction of your weak nature and His powerful presence. Ask for the light of God's Word to show you your true nature and sin, and God's forigivng heart even though he hates evil. Pray for forgiveness.

Remarkable Deliverances

20. ★ Thank God for His deliverance from sin and Christ's purchase of forgiveness for His people on the Cross at Calvary.
⌘ Ask God to show you in His Word the truth and the reality of Christ's suffering and death. Pray that you will come to know that it was for sinners He came to die and that He will convict you personally of your own sin.

21. ★ Thank God that there is no time when He sleeps or loses concentration. Trust in Him for continual and eternal protection.
⌘ Pray that God will protect you from giving into temptation. Pray that He will build a wall of protection around your soul and that you will submit your life to Him entirely.

22. ★ Thank God for His mercy. Ask Him for a desire to combat sin and its hold over you.
⌘ Ask God to make you merciful and ask forgiveness for those times that you have not forgiven others and have not helped when you could have.

23. ★ Thank God for salvation and forgiveness of sins. Ask Him to help you show others that Christ is the only cure for sin.
⌘ Ask God to lead you to Him for safety of your eternal soul and ask Him to convict you of the danger that you are in without Him.

24. ★ Ask God to give you a love for Him that is above all others and all else. Ask Him also that in His power and grace He will give you the ability to love others as you love yourself.

✠ Plead with God to take away your sinful desire. Ask Him to give you His love for others when you would rather love yourself instead.

25.　★ Thank God for His strength and provisions for you. Tell Him you love Him if He has given you this love. Thank Him for this gift.
✠ Ask God to show you how terrible a sinner you are and what a wonderful deliverance is available for all who trust in Jesus Christ and His blood shed on the Cross.

26.　★ Thank God for His protection during times when you didn't know you were in danger.
✠ Pray that God will convict you of sin and of His love and that He will bring you into the number of people that belong to Him.

27.　★ Thank God for His perfect plan. Cast your cares on Him. Rejoice that Christ's death means eternal life for His people.
✠ Ask God to show you how undeserving you are of His goodness and that how loving and wonderful He is to show you any mercy at all.

28.　★ Ask God to make you honest and trustworthy in all things and so reflect Christ's nature.
✠ Ask forgivness for the sin of unthankfulness. Ask God to show you your need of Him.

29.　★ Thank God for His salvation and for finding you and saving you.
✠ Ask God to show you your lost condition and the life-line Christ offers at Calvary.

30.　★ Thank God for the free access to himself through the sacrifice of His Son Jesus Christ.

⌘ Ask God to convict you of the sin of self-dependence. Ask Him to help you realize that salvation is received through Christ alone and that He is the only way to the Father.

31. ★ Thank Christ for His selfless sacrifice of becoming sin for His people.
⌘ Ask God to show you how beautiful and wonderful His son is. Ask Him to give you a sense of wonder at what the Son of God has done to gain salvation for the lost.

32. ★ Ask Christ to forgive you for the hurt you have caused Him. Thank Him from the bottom of your heart for saving and helping you by giving himself up to death, even death on the cross.
⌘ Ask God to show you your sins and transgressions and to show you what Jesus, the Lamb has done to save sinners like you.

33. ★ Ask God to forgive you for your sins and help you to defeat temptation.
⌘ Ask God to convict you of your sins and to save you from unrighteousness.

34. ★ Give God the glory for all He has done in your life.
⌘ Ask God to show you what is most important in your life and if it is not himself then ask God to change your heart to follow Him.

35. ★ Ask God to help you with your problems and ask Him to help you trust in Him for help.
⌘ Ask God to show you that your greatest problem is sin and your greatest need is Christ.

Scripture Index for Book 3

1. Luke 18:28-30

2. Proverbs 13:15
    Mark 12:42
    1 Timothy 6:3-16

3. 1 Kings 8:22-30

4. 1 Chronicles 29:14
    Luke 21:1-4
    Romans 12:1-21

5. Exodus 20:8
    Daniel 6
    2 John 9

6. Genesis 39
    1 Samuel 2:30; 1 Samuel 20

7. Exodus 20:15,16
    Proverbs 11:1-6

8. Exodus 20:8
    John 12:23-26; 21:6
    Jonah 1&2
    Matthew 8:23-27
    Acts 27

9. Deuteronomy 6:7
    Acts 24:25; 26:28
    Psalm 51:11
    Ezekiel 33:11
    John 3
    3 John 11
    Revelation 3:20

10. 1 John 5:3
    Exodus 16:13-31; 20:8-11

11. Acts 24:25; 26:28
    Hebrews 2:1-4

12. Exodus 20:7
    Leviticus 19:12
    Matthew 5:34
    James 3:10; 5:12

13. Deuteronomy 8:2
    Isaiah 26:34
    Acts 16:16-34

14. 2 Chronicles 7:14
    John 6:1-14

15. Ecclesiastes 11:9
    Psalm 133:1; 147:16
    Matthew 6:5-15
    Luke 22:17
    Acts 9:11
    James 5:16

16. 1 Kings 17
    John 21:1-4

17. 1 Kings 22
    Zephaniah 2:12-13
    Matthew 6:19-20; 16:26
    Hebrews 2:8

18. 2 Chronicles 24

19. Daniel 1:1-21
    Acts 16:25

20. Psalm 79:8 & 9; 80:3; 91
    Isaiah 55:11
    Daniel 3:1-20
    Matthew 4:6; 6:13

21. 2 Kings 7:13-23
    Matthew 10:29

22. Genesis 19:1-29
    Matthew 5:7

23. Isaiah 32:1-8
     John 19:34

24. Lamentations 3:22-23
     Psalm 89:1-10
     Obadiah 15
     Matthew 7:12; 19:19

25. Psalm 119:65-72

26. Psalm 124
     Proverbs 1:33

27. Isaiah 3:10
     Romans 8:28-39
     Hebrews 12:11

28. Acts 27
     Philippians 4:8

29. Acts 9:1-9
     Genesis 37:23-28
     Jeremiah 38

30. Hebrews 4:14-16

31. John 10:11-18

32. Isaiah 53:5
     John 1:29-34

33. Genesis 16
     Joshua 7
     Acts 5
     Jude 24

34. Genesis 41:1-45
     Acts 10:25; 14
     Romans 9:25-26

35. Psalm 34:15, 17,22; 50:15
     Judges 14:1-16

Answers

1. The fourth commandment. Exodus 20:8.
2. The Widow in Mark 12:42.
3. Discuss.
4. Discuss. Everything we have has been given to us by God anyway.
5. They do not abide in the doctrine of Christ and they do not have God.
6. He fled. Genesis 39.
7. Commandments 8 and 9, Exodus 15,16.
8. Jonah; The disciples; Paul. Jonah 1&2; Matthew 8:23-27; Acts 27.
9. Nicodemus. John 3. Follow not that which is evil but that which is good.
10. Six. He hallowed and blessed it.
11. Discuss.
12. The third commandment. Exodus 20:7.
13. Discuss.
14. Discuss.
15. Christ. Luke 22:17.
16. Elijah, the Widow, her son. 1 Kings 17.
17. No. Possessions don't last but your soul is eternal. Matthew 6:19-20. Their goods, houses, and vineyards will be destroyed.
18. Discuss.
19. Paul and Silas. Acts 16:25.
20. Sin; our sinful desires; snares or traps; troubles; diseases; terrors at night; attacks in the day; wars; evil; plagues; falling; wild beasts Psalm 91:11; Matthew 4:6; Temptation; Matthew 6:13—Deliver us from evil.
21. Sparrow. Matthew 10:29.
22 Matthew 5 - Blessed are the poor in spirit; Blessed are they that mourn; Blessed are the

meek; Blessed are they which do hunger and thirst after righteousness; Blessed are the merciful; Blessed are the pure in heart; Blessed are the peacemakers; Blessed are they which are persecuted for righteousness' sake; Blessed are ye when men shall revile you, and persecuite you, and shall say all manner of evil against you falsely, for my sake.

23   Crucifixion. John 19:34.

24.   Love them as ourselves. Matthew 19:19.The day of the Lord is near for all nations. As you have done, it will be done to you; your deeds will return on your own head. Obadiah 15. Do to others what you would have them do to you.   Matthew 7:12. He   might have stopped and helped the woman and her child.

25.   From a crocodile and a tiger and from eternal death through the redeeming blood of Jesus Christ.

26.   Covenanters and Scotland.
They shall be kept safe and not be afraid of evil.

27.   The righteous. Isaiah 3:10.
It saved him from a death sentence.

28.   Honest. Philippians 4:8.

29.   Joseph and Jeremiah. Genesis 37:23-28; Jeremiah 38.
If you don't know you are lost you don't realize your need of Christ.

30.   Through Jesus Christ his Son.

31   A disregard for God's Word and getting into bad company: The Word of God.

32.   Prophecy.

33.   Achan; Joshua. Annanias and Saphira; Acts 5. Being presented faultless before the presence of God's glory with exceeding joy.

34.   Peter;Acts 10:25. Paul; Barnabas; Acts 14

35.   The Righteous. Psalm 34:15.

Building on the Rock
Books 1-5

If you enjoyed this book:

Book 3
How God Used a Snowdrift
Honoring God and Dramatic Deliverances

You will also enjoy these other
titles by Joel R Beeke
and Diana Kleyn

Book 1
How God Used a Thunderstorm
Virtuous living and The Value of Scripture

Book 2
How God Stopped the Pirates
*Missionary Tales and
Remarkable Conversions*

Book 4
How God Used a Drought and an
Umbrella
Faithful Witnesses and Childhood Faith

Book 5
How God Sent a Dog
to Save a Family
God's Care and Childhood Faith

Other books published by Christian
Focus Publications in connection with
Reformation Heritage Books.

A First Catechism by Carine Mackenzie
and Teachers' Manual by Diana Kleyn

Doctrines and subjects covered in
thesc two titles include:
God
Creation
How man sinned
What happened because of sin
Salvation
Jesus as Prophet, Priest and King
The Ten Commandments
Keeping God's Laws
The way to be Saved
Experiencing God's salvation
Baptism and the Lord's Supper
Prayer
Where is Jesus now?
Death
Hcll
Heaven

Classic Devotions by F.L. Mortimer

Use these books alongside an open Bible and you will learn more about characters such as Cain and Abel, Abraham, Moses and Joshua, amongst others. You will enjoy the discussion generated and the time devoted to devotions and getting into God's Word. Investigate the Scriptures and build your knowledge with question and answer sessions with F. L. Mortimer's range of classic material. Written over a hundred years ago, this material has been updated to include activities and discussion starters for today's family.

ISBN: 1-85792-5858
         1-85792-5866
         1-85792-5912

The Complete Classic Range: Worth Collecting

A Basket of Flowers 1-85792-5254
Christie's Old Organ 1-85792-5238
A Peep Behind the Scenes 1-85792-5254
Little Faith 1-85792-567X
Mary Jones and Her Bible 1-85792-5688
Saved at Sea 1-85792-795-8
Children's Stories by D L Moody
1-85792-640-4
Children's Stories by J C Ryle
1-85792-639-0
Childhood's Years 1-85792-713-3